"And how do I live, Olivia?"

"You know as well as I do. Parties till dawn and a different woman in your bed every night."

"You disapprove."

"It's not for me to judge, but it's certainly not how I want to live my life."

"Surely there's a balance? We're opposites, you and I, in our pursuit of pleasure, but don't you think we could find some middle ground?"

Her eyes flashed. "And where would that be?"

In bed. Aziz had a sudden, vivid image of Olivia lying on top of tangled satin sheets, her glorious hair spread out on the pillow, her lips rosy and swollen from his kisses. His libido stirred insistently. He knew he had no business thinking like this, feeling like this.

And yet he did.

Rivals to the Crown of Kadar

Ruthless in battle, ruthless in love...

Two powerful men locked in a struggle to rule the country of their birth...

One a desert prince, once banished and shamed, the other a royal playboy cutting a swath through the beautiful women of Europe.

Tortured by their memories of the past, these bitter enemies will use any means necessary to win...but neither expected the women who would change the course of their revenge!

You read Khalil's story in
Captured by the Sheikh
September 2014

Now read Aziz's story in
Commanded by the Sheikh
October 2014

Kate Hewitt

—

Commanded by the Sheikh

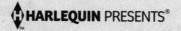
HARLEQUIN PRESENTS®

Recycling programs
for this product may
not exist in your area.

ISBN-13: 978-0-373-13282-9

COMMANDED BY THE SHEIKH

First North American Publication 2014

Copyright © 2014 by Kate Hewitt

HARLEQUIN®

Printed in U.S.A.

www.Harlequin.com

All about the author...
Kate Hewitt

KATE HEWITT discovered her first Harlequin® romance novel on a trip to England when she was thirteen, and she's continued to read them ever since. She wrote her first story at the age of five, simply because her older brother had written one and she thought she could do it, too. That story was one sentence long—fortunately, they've become a bit more detailed as she's grown older.

She studied drama in college and shortly after graduation moved to New York City to pursue a career in theater. This was derailed by something far better—meeting the man of her dreams, who happened also to be her older brother's childhood friend. Ten days after their wedding they moved to England, where Kate worked a variety of different jobs—drama teacher, editorial assistant, youth worker, secretary and, finally, mother.

When her oldest daughter was one year old, Kate sold her first short story to a British magazine. Since then she has sold many stories and serials, but writing romance remains her first love—of course!

Besides writing, she enjoys reading, traveling and learning to knit—it's an ongoing process, and she's made a lot of scarves. After living in England for six years, she now resides in Connecticut with her husband, her three young children and, possibly one day, a dog.

Kate loves to hear from readers. You can contact her through her website, www.kate-hewitt.com.

CHAPTER ONE

'I NEED YOU, OLIVIA.'

Olivia Ellis quickly suppressed the flare of feeling Sheikh Aziz al Bakir's simply stated words caused inside her. Of course he needed her. He needed her to change his sheets, polish his silver and keep his Parisian townhouse on the Ile de la Cité pristine.

That didn't explain what she was doing here, in the royal palace of Kadar.

Less than eight hours ago she'd been summoned by one of Aziz's men, asked unequivocally to accompany him on the royal jet to Siyad—the capital of Kadar—where Aziz had recently ascended the throne.

Olivia had gone reluctantly, because she liked the quiet life she'd made for herself in Paris: mornings with the concierge across the street sipping coffee, afternoons in the garden pruning roses. It was a life that held no excitement or passion, but it was hers and it made her happy, or as happy as she knew how to be. It was enough, and she didn't want it to change.

'What do you need of me, Your Highness?' she asked. She'd spent the endless flight to Kadar composing reasons why she should stay in Paris. She *needed* to stay in Paris, needed the safety and comfort of her quiet life.

'Considering the circumstances, I think you should

call me Aziz.' The smile he gave her was whimsical, effortlessly charming, yet Olivia tried to remain unmoved. She'd often observed Aziz's charm from a distance, had heard the honeyed words slide from his lips as he entertained one of his many female guests in Paris. She'd picked up the discarded lingerie from the staircase and had poured coffee for the women who crept from his bed before breakfast, their hair mussed and their lips swollen.

She, however, had always considered herself immune to 'the Gentleman Playboy', as the tabloids had nicknamed him. A bit of an oxymoron, Olivia thought, but she had to admit Aziz possessed a certain charisma.

She felt it now, with him focusing all of his attention on her, the opulent palace with its frescoed walls and gold fixtures stretching around them.

'Very well, Aziz. What do you need of me?' She spoke briskly, as she had when discussing replacing the roof tiles or the guest list for a dinner party. Yet it took a little more effort now, being in this strange and overwhelming place with this man.

He was, Olivia had to admit, beautiful. She could acknowledge that, just as she acknowledged that Michelangelo's *David* was a magnificent sculpture; it was nothing more than a simple appreciation of undeniable beauty. In any case, she didn't have anything left inside her to feel more than that. Not for Aziz, not for anyone.

She gazed now at the ink-black hair that flopped carelessly over his forehead; his grey eyes that could flare silver; the surprisingly full lips that could curve into a most engaging smile.

And as for his body…powerful, lean perfection, without an extra ounce of fat anywhere, just pure, perfect muscle.

Aziz steepled his fingers under his chin and turned towards the window so his back was partially to her. Olivia waited, felt the silence inexplicably tauten between them. 'You have been in my employ for six years now?' he said after a moment, his voice lilting as if it was a question, even though Olivia knew it was not.

'Yes, that's correct.'

'And I have been very pleased with your dedicated service in all of that time.'

She tensed. He sounded as if he were about to fire her. *And so now I'm afraid I have to tell you that I have no need of you any more...*

She took a careful breath, let it out silently. 'I'm very glad to hear that, Your Highness.'

'Aziz, remember.'

'Considering your status, it doesn't seem appropriate to call you by your first name.'

'Even if I demand it by royal decree?'

He turned around and raised his eyebrows, clearing teasing her. Olivia's mouth compressed. 'If you demand it, I shall of course comply,' she answered coolly. 'But in any case I shall do my best to call you by your first name.'

'I know you will. You have always done your best, Olivia, and that is exactly what I need from you today.'

She waited, unease creeping its cold fingers along her spine. What on earth could he need her for now, here in Kadar? She didn't like surprises or uncertainty; she'd spent six years creating something safe, small and good and she was terribly afraid of losing it. Of losing herself.

'In Paris you have done an admirable job keeping my home clean and comfortable and welcoming,' Aziz told her. 'I have another task entirely for you here, but it shall be short, and I trust you are capable of it.'

She had no idea what he was talking about, but if it

was short she hoped it meant that she'd be able to return to Paris, and soon. 'I hope that I am, Your—Aziz.'

He smiled, his gaze sweeping over her in approval. 'See what a quick learner you are?' he murmured.

Olivia said nothing. She ignored the little flutter of—something—Aziz's lazy murmur had caused inside her. In Paris their conversations were so mundane Olivia simply hadn't felt the full force of the Gentleman Playboy's charisma. That she should feel it here, now, was disconcerting but understandable. She was out of her element, in this beautiful yet overwhelming palace, and Aziz wasn't talking to her about house repairs or his social diary.

She gave him a quick, cool, professional smile. 'I'm afraid I still don't understand why I'm here.'

'All in good time.' Aziz flashed her an answering smile before walking over to a walnut desk inlaid with hand-tooled leather. He pressed a button on the side of the desk and within seconds Olivia heard a knock on the door.

'Enter,' Aziz said, and the same man who had escorted her to the room came in.

'Your Highness?'

Aziz braced one hip against the desk. 'What do you think, Malik? Will she do?'

Malik's gaze flicked to Olivia. 'The hair...'

Aziz snapped his fingers. 'Easily dealt with.'

'Eyes?'

'Not necessary.'

Malik nodded slowly. 'She's about the right height.'

'I thought so.'

The man turned to look at Aziz. 'Discreet?'

'Absolutely.'

'Then I think it's a possibility.'

'It's more than a possibility, Malik, it's a necessity. I'm holding a press conference in one hour.'

Malik shook his head. 'One hour—there won't be time.'

'There has to be. You know I can't risk any more instability.' Olivia watched as Aziz's expression shuttered, his mouth hardening into a grim line, turning him into someone utterly unlike the laughing, careless playboy she was familiar with. 'One rumour at this point will be like a lit match. Everything could go up in flames.'

'Indeed, Your Highness. I'll start making preparations.'

'Thank you.'

Malik withdrew and Olivia turned to Aziz. 'What on earth was all that about?'

'I apologise for speaking in such a way with Malik. I'm sure you are more confused than ever.'

'You're right,' Olivia answered, her voice coming out in something close to a snap. She hadn't liked the way the two men had discussed her...as if she were an object. She might be Aziz's housekeeper, but she wasn't his possession, and she had no intention of letting another person control her actions or attitude ever again.

'Pax, Olivia.' Aziz held up his hands. 'There would have been no point continuing our discussion if Malik hadn't approved of you.'

'*Approved* of me?'

'Found you suitable.'

'For what?'

Aziz let out a little sigh, the sound sudden. 'I presume you are not aware of the terms of my father's will?' he asked.

'No, I'm not,' Olivia replied. 'I'm not privy to such information, naturally.'

He shrugged, the movement careless, negligent, yet utterly graceful. 'It could have leaked out. There have been rumours of what the will requires.'

'I don't pay any attention to rumours.' She didn't even know what they were; she didn't read gossip magazines or tabloids.

Aziz lifted his eyebrows. 'You know I am engaged to Queen Elena of Thallia?'

'Yes, of course.' Their engagement had been announced publicly last week; Olivia knew the wedding was in the next few days, here in Kadar.

'You might have wondered why Queen Elena and I became engaged so quickly,' Aziz remarked, his dark gaze steady on her as he waited for her reaction.

Olivia gave a little shrug. Gentleman though he might be, Aziz was still a playboy. She'd seen the evidence herself in the women he'd brought home to his Paris house, had turned away more than one ardent admirer who'd received the diamond bracelet and bouquet of lilies that was Aziz's standard parting gift.

'I expect you feel a need to marry, now that you are Sheikh,' she said, and Aziz let out a little laugh, the sound hard, abrupt and utterly unlike him.

'You could say that.' He gazed out of the window once more, his lips pressed together in a firm line. 'My father has never approved of my choices,' he said after a moment. 'Or of me. I suspect the requirements of his will were put in place so he could keep me in Kadar, bound by the old traditions.' He lifted one shoulder in a shrug. 'Or perhaps he just wanted to punish me. That is perfectly possible.' He spoke easily, almost as if he was mentioning something pleasant or perhaps trivial, but she saw a coldness, or perhaps even a hurt, in his eyes.

Curiosity flickered and she quickly stamped it out.

She had no need to know about Aziz's relationship with his father, or with anyone. No need to wonder about what emotions he tried to hide, if any. 'What requirements?'

'In order to remain Sheikh, I must marry within six weeks of my father's death.' Aziz's mouth possessed a cynical twist, his eyes flinty. She'd never seen him look so bitter.

'It's been over a month already.'

'Exactly, Olivia. It has, in fact, been five weeks and four days. And my wedding to Queen Elena of Thallia is set for the day after tomorrow.'

'Then you will succeed,' she answered. 'You will marry within the time required and there'll be no problem.'

'But there is a problem,' Aziz informed her, his voice turning dangerously silky and soft. 'There is a big problem, because Elena has gone missing.'

'Missing?'

'Kidnapped by an insurgent two days ago.'

Olivia gaped before she managed to reassemble her features into her usual composed countenance. 'I had no idea things like this still happened in a civilised country.'

'You'd be surprised what can happen in any country, when power is involved. What secrets people keep, what lies they tell.' He swung away from her, the movement sudden, strangely defensive; again Olivia had the sense he was hiding something from her. Hiding himself.

In the six years she'd worked for him, Aziz had always seemed like nothing more than what he was on the surface: a charming, careless playboy. But for a moment, as he angled his face away from her, he seemed as if he had secrets. Darkness.

And she knew all about secrets and darkness.

'Do you know where this—this insurgent might be keeping Queen Elena?' Olivia asked after a moment.

'Somewhere in the desert, most likely.'

'And you're looking for her?'

'Of course, as best as I can.' Aziz turned around to meet her troubled gaze with an unflinching one of his own. 'I have not been back to Kadar in five years and I spent as little time here as a boy as possible. The people don't know me.' His mouth twisted. 'And, if they don't know me, they won't be loyal to me. Not until I've proved myself to them, if I can.'

'What are you saying—?' she began, only to have Aziz cut her off in a hard voice.

'I'm saying it is very difficult to find Queen Elena in the desert. Her kidnapper has the loyalty of the Bedouin tribes, and they will shelter both him and her. So until I find her, or come to some agreement with him, I need to make alternative arrangements.'

'What kind of alternative arrangements?' Olivia asked, although she had a horrible, creeping feeling just what they might be, or at least who they might concern. *Her.* Somehow he wanted to involve her in this debacle.

Aziz gave her a dazzling grin, his eyes flaring silver, his teeth blindingly white. Olivia felt her body involuntarily respond, her insides pulse with awareness of him, not as an employer or even an attractive person, a work of art, but as a man. A desirable man.

She blinked and forced back that rush of surprising, and completely inappropriate, feeling. Clearly it was just a basic biological reaction she had no control over. She had thought she was past such things, that she didn't have anything left in her to fizz or spark, but perhaps her body thought otherwise. Even so, her mind would prevail. 'Your Highness—'

'Aziz.'

'*Aziz*. What alternative arrangements are you talking about?'

'It is important that no one knows Elena is missing. Such knowledge would make Kadar more unstable than it already is.'

'*More* unstable?'

'Some of the desert tribes have rallied around this rebel.' Aziz's mouth twisted. 'Khalil.'

He spoke tersely, without emotion, yet Olivia still sensed something underneath his flat tone, something that seethed. Who exactly, she wondered, was Khalil?

'Why have they rallied around this Khalil? You're the legal heir.'

'Thank you for your vote of confidence, but I'm afraid it's a bit more complicated than that.'

He spoke lightly again, but Olivia wasn't fooled. 'How is it complicated? And what could I possibly have to do with any of this?'

'Since I can't let the public know my bride is missing,' Aziz said, turning the full force of his silvery gaze on her once more, 'I need someone else.'

Olivia felt as if someone had caught her by the throat and squeezed. For a moment she couldn't breathe. 'Someone else,' she finally repeated, her voice coming out flat and strange.

'Yes, Olivia. Someone else. Someone to be my bride.'

'But—'

'And that's where you come in.' Aziz cut her off smoothly, something almost like amusement glinting in his eyes. Olivia stared at him, disbelieving and appalled. 'I need you to be my bride.'

CHAPTER TWO

HIS COOL, CAPABLE HOUSEKEEPER, Aziz thought in bemusement, looked as if she was about to hyperventilate. Or faint. She swayed slightly, her lovely slate-blue eyes going wider, her lush, pink lips parted in a rather delectable *o*.

She was a beautiful woman, he acknowledged as he had many times before, but it was a cool, contained beauty. Sleek, caramel hair she always kept clipped back at the base of her neck. Dark blue eyes. Smooth skin and rosy lips, neither ever enhanced by make-up, at least that he'd seen. Not that she needed any cosmetics, particularly right now. A flush was rising up her throat, sweeping across her face as she shook her head and compressed her mouth.

'I'm not quite sure what you even mean, Your Highness, but whatever it is it's not possible.'

'To start with, you need to remember to call me Aziz.'

Temper blazed so briefly in her eyes he almost missed it. He was glad, contrarily, perhaps, that she actually possessed a temper. He'd often wondered how much passion lurked beneath that reserved exterior.

He'd known Olivia for six years, admittedly seeing her only a few times a year, and he'd had only a scant few glimpses of any deeper feeling. A silk scarf in deep reds and purples that he'd been surprised to see her wear.

A sudden rich, full-throated laugh he'd heard from the kitchen. Once, when he'd arrived in Paris a day early, he'd come upon her playing piano in the sitting room. The music had been haunting, full of grief and beauty. And the look on her face as she'd played... She'd been pouring her soul into that piece of music, and it was, he'd thought in that moment, a soul that had known anguish and even torment.

He'd crept away before she'd seen him, knowing how horrified she would have been to realise he'd been listening. But he'd wondered just what lay underneath her cool façade. What secrets she might be hiding.

And yet it was her cool façade, her calm capability, that had made him choose Olivia Ellis for this particular role. She was intelligent, discreet and wonderfully competent. That was all he needed.

He hoped.

'Let me rephrase,' he said, watching as her chest rose and fell in indignant breaths. She wore a white blouse that still managed to be crisp after a nine-hour flight from Paris, and her hair, as sleek and styled as ever, was held back in its usual clip. She'd matched her blouse with a pair of tailored black trousers and sensible flats. He knew she was twenty-nine but she dressed conservatively, like a woman who was middle-aged rather than in the prime of her youth. Though still stylish, he acknowledged. Her clothes, while staid, were of good quality and cut.

'Rephrase, then,' she said evenly, and the temper he'd seen in her eyes was now banked. He saw the old Olivia, the familiar Olivia, return now. Calm and in control. *Good.* That was what he needed, after all.

So why did he feel just a tiny bit disappointed?

'I need you to be my temporary bride. A stand-in for Queen Elena, until I can find her.'

'And why do you need a stand-in?'

'Because I want to dispel any rumours that she might be missing. I'm holding a press conference in one hour and we're meant to appear together on the palace balcony.'

She pursed her lips. 'And then?'

He hesitated, but only briefly. 'And then, that's all.'

'That's all?' Her eyes narrowed. 'If you only needed a woman for one balcony appearance, surely you could have found someone a bit more local?'

'I wanted someone I knew and trusted and, as I told you before, I have not been back to Kadar in many years. There are few I trust here.'

She swallowed and he watched the working of her slender throat. Then she gave a little shake of her head.

'I don't even look like Queen Elena. She's got dark hair and we're not the same height, no matter what you said earlier to your staff. I must be a few inches taller.'

He arched an eyebrow. 'You're familiar with Queen Elena's height?'

'I'm familiar with my own,' she answered coolly. 'And I have seen photos of her. I'm guessing, of course, but—'

'No one will concern themselves with a few inches.'

'And my hair?'

'We'll dye it.'

'In the next *hour*?'

'If need be.'

She stared at him for a long beat, and he felt tension gather inside him in a tight, hard knot. He knew he was making an unusual request, to say the least. He also knew he had to get Olivia to agree. He didn't want to threaten her, God knew, but he needed her. He didn't have any other woman in his life who he trusted to be discreet and competent, the way Olivia was. He supposed that said something about his own life, but at this moment all he could care about was achieving his goal. Securing the crown of a kingdom he'd been born to rule…even if many didn't believe it. Even if he'd never been sure he would.

Never sure if his father would change his mind and disinherit him, just as he had Khalil.

'And if I say no?' Olivia asked and Aziz gave her his most charming smile.

'But why would you?'

'Because it's insanity?' she shot back without a shred of humour. 'Because any paparazzi with a telephoto lens could figure out I'm not Queen Elena and plaster it all over the tabloids? I don't think even the Gentleman Playboy could charm himself out of that disaster.'

'So cutting, Olivia.' He shook his head in gentle mockery. 'If that happened, I'd be responsible. All the blame would fall to me.'

'You don't think I'd be dragged through the gossip mill, every aspect of my life dissected in the tabloids?' For a second her features contorted, as if such a possibility caused her actual physical pain. *'No.'*

'*If* you were discovered, which you won't be,' Aziz answered calmly, 'No one would who know you are.'

'You don't think they could find out?'

'Possibly, but we're theorising to no purpose. There are no journalists out there. The country has been closed to foreign press for years. I have yet to change that decree.'

'The Kadaran press, then.'

'Have always been in the royal pocket. I've requested no photographs on this occasion, and they'll comply.' His insides tightened. 'I'm not condoning the way things are here, but it's how my father ran things, and currently it continues.'

She stared at him for a moment, her slate-blue gaze

searching his face. 'Are you going to do things differently now you're Sheikh?' She sounded curious but also a bit disbelieving, which Aziz could understand, even if he didn't like it.

He hadn't proved himself capable of much besides being a whiz with numbers and partying across Europe, at least to someone like Olivia. She'd seen his hedonistic lifestyle first-hand, had cleaned up its excesses. He could hardly blame her now for being a little sceptical of his ability to rule well, or even at all.

'I'm going to try.'

'And you'll start with this ridiculous masquerade.'

'I'm afraid it's necessary.' He cocked his head, offering her a smile that didn't even make her blink. 'It's for a good reason, Olivia. The stability of a country. The safety of a people.'

'Why has Khalil kidnapped Queen Elena? And how did he even do it? Wasn't she guarded?'

A hot, bright flare of anger fired his insides. Aziz didn't know whom that anger was directed at: Khalil, for taking his bride, or his staff, who had not been alert to the threat until it was too late. No, he realised, he was angry at himself, even though he knew he could not have prevented the kidnapping. He was angry that he couldn't have prevented it, that he didn't know this country or people well enough yet to command their loyalty or obedience—or to find Elena hidden somewhere in its endless, barren desert.

'Khalil is the illegitimate son of my father's first wife,' he explained tersely. 'He was raised as my father's son for seven years, until my father discovered the truth of his parentage. My father banished him, along with his mother, but he insists now that he has a claim to the throne.'

'How awful.' Olivia shook her head. *'Banished.'*

'He was raised in luxury by his aunt in America,' Aziz told her. 'You needn't feel sorry for him.'

She eyed him curiously. 'You obviously don't.'

Aziz just shrugged. What he felt for Khalil—when he even allowed himself to think of the man who shadowed his memories like a malevolent ghost—was too complicated to explain even to himself, much less to Olivia. Anger and envy. Sorrow and bitterness. A potent and unhealthy mix, to say the least.

'I admit,' he said, 'I don't have much sympathy for him now, considering he is destabilising my country and has kidnapped my bride.'

'Why do you think he believes he has a right to the throne?'

Because everyone else does. Because my father adored him, even when he learned he wasn't his son. Even when he didn't want to. 'I'm not sure he does believe he has a right,' he told her with a small shrug. 'This might just be revenge against my father, a man he thought to be his own father for much of his childhood.' Aziz glanced away from Olivia's inquisitive gaze. *Revenge against me, for taking his place.* 'My father was not a fair man. This extraordinary will is surely proof of that.'

'And so Khalil has kidnapped Queen Elena in order to prevent your marriage,' she stated slowly, and Aziz nodded, his jaw bunching. He hated to think of Queen Elena out in the desert, alone and afraid. He didn't know his prospective bride very well, but he could only imagine how terrifying such an experience would be for anyone, and especially for someone with her history. She'd told him a little of how her parents had died, how alone she'd been. He just hoped Khalil would keep her safe now.

'If you don't marry within the six weeks,' Olivia asked, 'What happens?'

'I lose the throne and title.'

'And who does it go to?'

Aziz hesitated. 'The will doesn't specify a particular person,' he answered. 'But a referendum will have to be called.'

'A referendum? You mean the people will decide who is Sheikh?'

'Yes.'

Her mouth curved slightly. 'That sounds nicely democratic.'

'Kadar has a constitutional monarchy,' Aziz answered, struggling to keep his voice even, dispassionate. 'The succession has always been dynastic. The referendum is simply my father's way of forcing me to jump through his hoops.'

'And you don't want to jump?'

'Not particularly, but I recognise the need.' He'd spent over three weeks trying to find a loophole in his father's will. He didn't want to marry, didn't want to be forced to marry, and certainly not by his father. His father had controlled his actions, his thoughts and desires for far too long.

Yet even in death his father had the power to control him. To hurt him. And here he was, jumping through hoops.

'Why not just call the referendum?' Olivia asked.

'Because I'd lose.' Aziz spoke easily, lightly, using the tone he'd taken for so long it was second nature to him—a second skin, this playboy persona of his. But talking about his father—about the possibility of Khalil being Sheikh because his country didn't want him—was making that second skin start to peel away, and he was afraid of what Olivia might be able to see through the tatters. 'Hazard of not spending much time in Kadar, I'm afraid,' he continued in a mocking drawl. 'But I'm hoping to remedy that shortly.'

'But not in time for the referendum.'

'Exactly. Which is why I need to appear with my bride and reassure my people that all is well.' He took a step towards her, willing her to understand, to accept. 'My father left his country in turmoil, Olivia, divided by the choices he made twenty-five years ago. I am trying my hardest to right those wrongs and keep Kadar in peace.'

He saw a flash of something in her slate-blue eyes—understanding, or even compassion. He was getting to her. He hoped. 'And if you don't find Queen Elena?' she asked.

'I will. I just need a little more time. I have men searching the desert as we speak.'

It had all been so cleverly, capably done. Khalil had planted a man loyal to him in Aziz's new staff, a man who had given Aziz the message that Elena's plane had been delayed by bad weather. He'd bribed the pilot of the royal jet to divert the flight to a remote desert location and he'd had his men meet Elena as she came off the plane.

That much he knew, had pieced together from witnesses: from the steward who had helplessly watched Elena disappear into a blacked-out SUV; the maid who had seen one of Aziz's staff looking secretive and shifty, loitering in places he shouldn't have been.

Aziz sighed. Yes, it had been capably done, because Khalil still had the loyalty of many of the Kadaran people. Never mind that he'd left Kadar when he'd been seven years old and had only returned to the country in the last six months. They remembered the young boy they'd known as Sheikh Hashem's beloved son—the real son, or so the whispers went.

Aziz was the interloper. The pretender.

He always had been, from the moment he'd been brought to the palace at just four years old. He remembered the way the staff had pretended not to hear his mother's humble requests, how they'd sneered even as they'd served them. He'd been bewildered, his mother desperate. She'd stopped trying to please anyone and had remained isolated in the women's quarters, rarely seen in public.

Aziz had tried. He had tried to win over the staff, the people and most of all his father. He'd failed in nearly every respect, and most definitely in the last. And so, finally, he'd stopped trying.

Except now. Now you want to try again. You're just afraid you'll fail.

He silenced the sly whisper of his personal demons and retrained his gaze on Olivia. They now had only forty minutes until his press conference. He had to make her agree.

'If I can't find Queen Elena, I'll arrange a meeting with Khalil. We might be able to negotiate.' Although Aziz didn't want to talk to Khalil, or even see him. Just the memory of the last time he'd seen Khalil made his stomach churn. The boy he'd thought was his half-brother had looked at him, all of four years old, as if he were something sticky and disgusting on the bottom of his shoe. Then his father had steered Aziz out of the royal nursery, dismissing him so he could be with the son he'd always favoured. The one he'd preferred, even when he'd learned that they shared no blood.

His father might have banished Khalil, but he'd chosen to cling to his memory and revile the son he'd made heir out of necessity rather than desire.

Now Aziz forced the memories back and turned to Olivia. 'In any case, none of that needs to concern you.

All I'm asking is that you appear on the balcony for about two minutes. People will see you from afar and be satisfied.'

'How can you be sure?'

'They're expecting Elena. They'll see Elena. I made the announcement that she arrived by royal jet this afternoon.'

She pursed her lips. 'When, in fact, I did.'

'Exactly. People will be waiting to see her. They're most likely lining the courtyard right now. Two minutes, Olivia, that's all I ask. And then you can return to Paris.'

She shook her head slowly. 'For how long?'

'What do you mean?'

'Will you really need a house in Paris with a full-time housekeeper once you're married and ruling Kadar, assuming you do find Queen Elena?'

He stared at her for a moment, nonplussed, before he realised she was worried about her job. 'I intend on keeping my house in Paris,' he told her, even though he hadn't actually considered it either way. 'And, as long as I have my house, you will have a job there.'

He saw relief flicker over her features, softening her eyes and mouth, relaxing the stiffness of her posture. She'd really been worried about her job.

'So? We are agreed?'

She shook her head, her eyes narrowed, the corners of her mouth pulled down. 'I don't...'

'I have forty minutes before I face the cameras and the reporters.' He took a step towards her, holding his hands out in appeal, offering the kind of wry smile he knew had melted hearts in the past, if not hers. 'You're my only hope, Olivia. My salvation. *Please*.'

Her mouth twitched before she firmed it into its usual

cool line. 'That might be laying it on a bit thick, Your Highness.'

'Aziz.'

She stared at him for a long moment and he could see the conflict clouding her eyes. Then she gave one brief nod, pulling herself up straight. 'All right,' she said quietly. 'I'll do it.'

CHAPTER THREE

WITHIN SECONDS MALIK had returned to the room and Aziz was speaking to him in rapid Arabic. Olivia felt as if she'd entered into some alternate reality. How on earth could she actually impersonate Queen Elena?

She'd been reluctant to agree, but she also saw the wisdom in going along with Aziz's outrageous plan. Aziz held her livelihood in his hands and, while he hadn't outright bribed or blackmailed her, Olivia had still felt the tit-for-tat exchange he was offering: *do this and you'll have a job for as long as you want.*

And her job, the life she'd built for herself in Paris, was all she wanted now. All she hoped to have.

She wasn't entirely self-serving, though, she told herself as she followed Malik down several marble-floored corridors. She understood Aziz's dilemma and she didn't want to exacerbate the instability of his country or rule. She didn't know if pretending to be someone else actually would help things, but she supposed it would at least buy Aziz some time.

And hopefully no one would ever know and tomorrow she would be back in Paris.

'This way, Miss Ellis.'

Malik opened a door and ushered Olivia into a bedroom decorated in peach and cream. She glanced around

the sumptuous room, from the canopied bed with its
satin cover and pile of pillows, to the brocade sofas
and teakwood dressing table. It was a woman's room,
feminine and opulent, and she wondered who had last
stayed in it.

'Mada and Abra are here to help you prepare,' Malik
said and two smiling, sloe-eyed women stepped forward
shyly to greet her. 'I'm afraid they speak very little English,' Malik said in apology. 'But I trust you will be in
good hands.' With a brief nod, he turned and left Olivia
alone with the two women.

With smiles and shy nods they ushered her towards
the *en suite* bathroom, which if anything was even more
sumptuous than the bedroom, with a sunken marble tub,
a two-person shower and double sinks with what looked
like solid gold taps.

One of the women said something to her in Arabic,
and Olivia shook her head helplessly. 'I'm sorry, I don't
understand...'

Smiling, she indicated her own clothes and then gestured to the buttons of Olivia's blouse. The other woman
held up a bottle of hair dye and belatedly Olivia understood. She needed to undress so they could dye her hair.

Why was she doing this again? she wondered as she
slid off her blouse and trousers and then stood shivering
in just her bra and pants. She felt embarrassingly self-
conscious; she lived such a solitary life now, and she
couldn't remember the last time anyone but her doctor
had seen her in her underwear.

One of the women draped a towel around her shoulders
and the other laid out the preparations for the hair dye.

'What is your name?' Olivia asked the woman who
had given her the towel. She wished she knew a little
Arabic. Did Queen Elena know any?

The woman understood her question, for she smiled and ducked her head. 'Mada.'

'Thank you, Mada,' Olivia said and Mada gave her a lovely, gap-toothed smile before leading her towards the marble sink.

Olivia leaned over the sink, closing her eyes as Mada ran warm water over her head and then worked in the hair dye. She realised she hadn't even asked if it was a temporary colour. She hadn't had time properly to consider the ramifications of this charade, she acknowledged as the other woman, Abra, snapped a plastic cover over her hair and eased her up from the sink.

She hadn't had time to ask Aziz if it was even legal. Was impersonating someone—and especially a royal someone—a *crime*? What if she was arrested? What if someone twigged she wasn't Elena and sold the story to the foreign press?

They might uncover other secrets. She couldn't bear the thought of the world knowing her past, raking over her secrets, judging her. She judged herself harshly enough, God knew. She didn't need everyone else doing it too.

And her father, she thought, would be disgraced. After selling her soul to keep him from disgrace ten years ago, the thought that he might end up humiliated anyway gave her a surprising surge of savage satisfaction, and then more familiar rush of guilt.

One appearance. Two minutes. Then it would be over.

A few moments later Mada indicated that she should rise from where she'd been seated, waiting for the dye to set, and Olivia returned to the sink and bent her head so the women could rinse the dye from her hair.

She watched the water in the sink stream blue-black with the dye. When it finally went clear Abra eased her up again, and she stared at herself in the mirror in shock.

She looked completely different. Her skin seemed paler, her eyes deeper, darker and wider somehow. Her hair, her smooth, caramel-coloured hair, now framed her face in a damp, inky tousle. She didn't really look like Queen Elena, but neither did she look like herself. Perhaps from a distance she really would pass as the monarch.

Mada took her by the hand and led her back into the bedroom where clothes had been laid out: a dove-grey suit jacket and narrow skirt paired with an ivory silk blouse.

She dressed quickly, sliding on the gossamer-thin, sheer stockings first, and then the blouse and suit. Four-inch black stilettos heels completed the ensemble. Olivia hesitated; she always wore plain, sensible flats. The heels, she thought as she gazed down at them, felt too…sexy.

And that was not a word she wanted to associate with herself…or Aziz.

Next came hair and make-up; the women styled her newly dark hair in an elegant chignon, then did her face with subtle eye shadow, eyeliner, lipstick and blusher, all of it more than Olivia ever wore. The clothes had been familiar but the shoes, make-up and hair made her feel strange. An impostor.

Which was exactly what Aziz wanted her to be—a convincing one.

A knock sounded on the door and then Malik entered. 'You are ready, Miss Ellis?'

She nodded stiffly. 'As ready I can be, I suppose.'

He glanced up and down her body and then nodded, seemingly in approval. 'Please come with me.'

As she followed him down the corridor, her heels clicking smartly on the marble tile, she remarked with a touch of acerbity, 'Clearly Mada and Abra are both in on this plan, and both of them looked far more like Queen Elena than I do. They have the right colouring, at least. Why couldn't one of them act as her stand-in?'

Malik slid her a sideways glance. 'Neither of those women possesses the confidence or ability to enact such a masquerade. In any case, they would not even be comfortable wearing Western clothes.'

'But you trust them? Aziz trusts them?'

Malik nodded. 'Yes, of course. Very few people know about this deception, Miss Ellis. Only you, Sheikh Aziz, myself, Mada and Abra.'

'And the crew of the royal jet,' Olivia pointed out. 'Plus the staff who escorted me here.'

He inclined his head in acknowledgement. 'True, but it is a contained group, and everyone in it is loyal to the Sheikh.'

'Aziz said he had not been in Kadar long enough to gain the people's loyalty.'

Malik gazed at her with an inscrutable expression. 'So he seems to think. But there are more loyal to Aziz than he knows, or allows himself to believe.'

Before Olivia could consider a response to that rather cryptic remark, Malik opened a door and ushered her into an ornate reception room. French windows led out to a wide balcony, and even from across the room Olivia was able to glimpse the courtyard below already filled with people pressed shoulder to shoulder, all of them craning their necks to catch a glimpse of their new Sheikh and his future bride.

Her stomach lurched and she pressed a hand to her mouth.

'Please don't be sick,' Aziz remarked dryly as he stepped into the room. 'That would ruin quite a lovely outfit.' He stopped in front of her, his silvery-grey gaze wandering up and down her figure, eyes gleaming with a blatant masculine approval that made Olivia's stomach tighten. He'd never looked at her like that before. 'Dark hair suits you. So do high heels.' His mouth quirked in a smile. 'Very much so. I'm almost sorry it's only a temporary dye.'

She lifted her chin, forcing the feeling back that Aziz stirred so easily up inside her. Why was she reacting to him now, when she never had before? 'As long as I look like Queen Elena. As much as I can, at any rate.'

'I think you'll pass. Very well, actually.' His smile turned sympathetic. 'I do recognise that I am asking much of you, Olivia. Your willingness to help me is deeply appreciated, believe me.'

Olivia met his compassionate gaze with a direct one of her own. 'I just want to return to Paris.'

'And so you shall. But first, the balcony.' He nodded towards the doors; even from here, with them closed, Olivia could hear the muted roar of the crowd below. She swallowed hard.

'You had the press conference?'

'Just a few moments ago.'

'Were the media concerned with why Queen Elena wasn't there?'

'A few asked, but I said you were tired from your journey and preparing to meet your new people. They accepted it. In any case, it would be unusual in this country for a woman to appear in front of the media and speak for herself.'

'But Queen Elena has spoken for herself many times,' Olivia observed. 'She's a reigning monarch.'

'True, but in Kadar she is merely going to be the wife of a Sheikh. There is a difference.'

Olivia heard a surprising edge of bitterness in his

voice and wondered at it. 'Why did Queen Elena agree to this marriage if she would have few rights in your country? It wasn't, I presume, a love match?'

'Indeed not.' Aziz flashed her a quick, hard smile. 'The alliance suited us both, for different reasons.'

A surprisingly implacable note had entered Aziz's voice, but Olivia ignored it. 'You speak in the past tense. Does it not still suit you?'

'It will,' Aziz told her. 'When I find her. But as for now...' He gestured to the balcony doors. 'Our adoring public awaits.'

Nerves coiled tightly in Olivia's belly and she nodded. There was surely no going back now. 'All right.'

'It is important for you to know,' Aziz said in a low voice as they walked towards the balcony, 'That, though my marriage to Elena was for convenience only, the public assumed it was a love match. They want it to be a love match.'

Olivia shot him a sharp glance, nerves leaping now, like a nest of snakes had taken up residence in her stomach. 'Even though you only became engaged a few weeks ago?'

Aziz shrugged. 'People believe what they want to believe.'

That, she thought grimly, had certainly been true in her own experience. 'So what does this mean for our appearance out there?'

Aziz gave her a teasing smile and reached out to brush her cheek with his fingers, sending a sudden shower of sparks cascading through Olivia's senses. Instinctively she jerked back. 'Only that we both need to act as if we are hopelessly in love. Try to restrain yourself from too much PDA, though, Olivia. This is a conservative country, after all.'

She opened her mouth in outrage, knowing he was joking yet still indignant. Aziz just chuckled softly then slipped his arm through hers and guided her out onto the balcony and the throng that waited below.

A cheer went up as soon as they both stepped outside; the hot, still air hit Olivia full in the face. She blinked, dumbfounded by the roar of approval that sounded from below and seemed to go on and on.

Aziz slid a hand around her waist, his fingers splayed across her hip as he raised one hand in greeting.

'Wave,' he murmured and obediently Olivia raised her hand. 'Smile,' he added, a hint of laughter in his voice, and she curved her lips upwards.

They stood like that, hip to hip, Aziz's hand around her waist, waving as the crowd continued to cheer.

'I thought,' Olivia said in a whisper, even though no one could possibly hear, 'That you said the Kadaran people were not loyal to you.'

He shrugged. 'They are a romantic people as well as a traditional one. They like the idea of my marriage, of a fairy-tale wedding, more than they like me.'

'It is indeed a fairy tale,' Olivia answered tartly and Aziz just smiled.

After another endless minute he dropped his hand. Olivia thought they would be finally, thankfully heading back inside, but he stayed her with his hand still around her waist, the other coming up to frame her jaw.

'What are you doing?' she hissed.

'The crowd wants to see us kiss.'

'What happened to no PDA?' she retorted through gritted teeth. 'And this being a conservative country?'

'Siyad is a little more modern. And we'll keep it chaste, don't worry. No tongues,' he advised, and as her mouth dropped open in shock he kissed her.

Olivia froze beneath the touch of his lips; it had been so long since she'd been kissed she'd forgotten how it felt—how intimate, strange and frankly wonderful. Aziz's lips were cool and soft, the hand that framed her face both tender and firm. Her eyes closed instinctively as she fought against the tidal wave of want that crashed so unexpectedly through her.

'There.' He eased back, smiling. 'You managed to restrain yourself.'

'Easily,' she snapped, and he laughed softly.

'It's so delightfully simple to get a rise out of you, Olivia. It makes your eyes sparkle.'

'How *delightful* to know,' Olivia retorted, and he just laughed again.

'Indeed.'

He was leading her back inside but Olivia was barely aware of her surroundings. Her mind spun with sensation and her lips buzzed, as if his brief kiss had electrocuted her. It had been an appropriately chaste kiss, little more than a brushing of mouths, yet her insides felt alarmingly shivery and weak. Why had a simple kiss affected her so much?

Because it hadn't been simple for her. When you hadn't been kissed in nearly a decade, Olivia thought, a little one like that could be explosive. Unforgettable.

It surely had nothing to do with *Aziz*. Although she had to admit that, in her limited experience at least, he seemed a very good kisser.

As soon as the balcony doors were closed, Olivia tugged her hand from Aziz's. 'There.' She fought the urge to wipe her mouth, as if such a childish action could banish the memory of his kiss and the unwelcome feelings it had stirred up inside her. 'We're done. I can go back to Paris.'

'And so you shall, in the morning.'

'Why not tonight?'

'It's a long flight, Olivia. The pilot needs to rest; the plane to be refuelled. Besides, I am meant to be having dinner with my bride, and I know you don't want to miss that.'

She ignored the teasing, even though part of her actually was tempted to smile. The man was incorrigible, determinedly so. 'You never said anything about dinner.'

'It must have slipped my mind.'

'Liar.'

'As Sheikh, I'm in control of how much information to disseminate at a given time, it's true.'

'Such big words.'

'I looked them up in the dictionary.'

And then she did smile, helpless to keep herself from it, knowing that she, like every other woman, was falling prey to his charm. 'And I'm meant to be Queen Elena at this dinner?'

'It's a private dinner, so you only have to pretend for me.'

'And the staff who see us together,' Olivia pointed out. 'Aziz, this is ludicrous. I might be able to pass myself off as Queen Elena from a balcony, but I can hardly do so face to face. One look at me and your staff will know.'

'You are assuming they will be suspicious,' Aziz answered calmly. 'And why should they be? Word went out that Queen Elena arrived by royal jet this afternoon. And so she did. Then she appeared with me on the balcony, as planned. Everything is going just as it should, Olivia. No one has reason to suspect otherwise.'

'Except for the fact that I don't look anything like her.'

'Do you think anyone here has seen Queen Elena in the flesh?'

'Photographs in the papers,' she argued. 'And, in any case, didn't she come here to discuss your marriage?'

Aziz nodded, still unruffled. 'Yes, but it was a private meeting, very discreet. At that point, neither of us wanted to make the negotiations public.'

'Even so.'

He smiled, laid a hand over hers, and Olivia had to fight the urge to yank her hand away. She'd been numb for so long, she hadn't thought she had any feelings or desires left for Aziz to stir up inside her. Yet he had. So easily, he had. 'Just dinner, Olivia. And then you can leave in the morning.'

She shook her head again, feeling as if she'd been caught in a riptide. She was being carried away from everything she'd known and wanted, everything *safe*, so quickly. She couldn't fight against it.

And yet she was honest enough to admit she was tempted—tempted to enjoy this fleeting time with Aziz, to let herself fall just a little bit under his spell. Just for a night. Then she'd go back to her little life.

'You need to eat, Olivia,' he murmured.

'I could have a sandwich in my room.'

'Fine, then I'll join you. Of course, then the staff might really gossip.'

She pulled her hand from his. 'You're impossible.'

He smiled and inclined his head. 'Thank you.'

'It wasn't,' she informed him tartly, 'A compliment.'

His smile just widened. 'I know.'

What point was there in resisting? Olivia wondered. Aziz would wear her down eventually with his tireless charm that masked a far more steely sense of purpose. She hadn't realised that before, hadn't seen how determined he could be, but then they'd never been at cross purposes before. And were they even now?

You are tempted...

Tempted to enjoy one evening with a beautiful man. Tempted to access those deadened parts of herself and feel like a beautiful, desirable woman, even if it was just pretend.

'Fine,' she said. 'I'll have dinner with you. But I leave first thing in the morning.'

She gazed at him in challenge and Aziz just smiled blandly. 'Of course,' he answered, and with a creeping sense of foreboding Olivia wondered if she dared to take him at his word—or if she even wanted to.

CHAPTER FOUR

THE PRIVATE DINING ROOM, one of the palace's smaller ones, had been set for a romantic dinner for two. Aziz raised an eyebrow at the snowy linen tablecloth, the creamy candles casting flickering shadows across the dim, wood-panelled room. Olivia, he knew, would not be pleased by any of it. He'd never met a woman so resistant to his charm.

Although, she hadn't been resistant when he'd kissed her. He'd felt her shock first, tensing her whole body as if a wire that ran through her had been jerked taut, and then he'd felt her compliance, even her desire, as her body had relaxed and her hand had come up to grip his shoulder. He wondered if she'd even been aware of the fullness of her response, how she'd drawn him closer, parted her lips under his. He'd teased her that she'd have to restrain herself but he hadn't thought she'd take him at his word.

And as she'd responded he'd felt, with a sudden, shocking urgency, a desire or even a need to deepen that kiss, slide his tongue into her mouth and taste her velvety sweetness.

Thank God he hadn't acted on that overwhelming instinct. The people of Siyad might want to see them kiss chastely; they would have been appalled by such a blatant display of sexual desire.

And what he'd felt for Olivia in that moment had been deeply, potently sexual. A complication, he mused, that he certainly didn't need right now.

'Your Highness.' A member of staff opened the doors of the dining room. 'Her Highness, Queen Elena.'

So she'd fooled at least one person, Aziz thought with satisfaction. Olivia stepped into the room, her dark hair styled into an ornate twist with a few tendrils curling around her face. She wore an evening gown of shimmering silver; the sparkling bodice hugged her tiny waist before flaring out around her legs in gossamer folds. She looked magnificent, radiant, and more beautiful than he'd ever seen her before. Lust reached out and caught him by the throat, left him momentarily breathless and blindsided.

The doors closed behind her and she stopped in front of them, fixing him with a defiant stare. 'I didn't choose this dress,' she told him. 'But Mada and Abra insisted. I don't even know where it came from.'

'I had some clothes ordered.'

'For the impostor or the real thing?' she retorted.

Aziz kept his own voice deliberately mild. 'Does it matter?'

'I don't know.' She looked lost for a moment, vulnerability melting the ice in her eyes, before she shook her head in weary resignation. 'This is all so strange.'

'I agree. But strange, in its own way, can be enjoyable.' Aziz walked towards her, wanting to touch her. He felt the entirely primal and primitive reaction of a man alone with a beautiful woman; he wanted to enjoy it, enjoy her, and not discuss how strange or wrong or dangerous it all was.

'You certainly look the part now,' he said as he gestured to her sparkling dress. 'You are lovely, Olivia.'

Her cheeks pinked and she arched one elegant eyebrow. 'I think you're a little more adept with the compliments than that.'

A smile tugged at his mouth. 'Oh, am I?'

'I've heard you compare a woman to a rose petal before.'

'Oh dear, that sounds rather uninspired.'

'She obviously fell for it. The two of you were upstairs before dessert was served.'

'Mmm.' He felt strangely disconcerted. He wasn't ashamed of his sexual exploits; he'd discovered at fifteen that women liked him, and after an isolated, unhappy childhood that had been a powerful aphrodisiac. So, maybe they only liked his body, his charm, but that was enough.

He wasn't looking to offer his heart. He knew what happened when you did that. He'd put his on a damn plate for most of his childhood, for anyone to shove away, to shatter.

Yet he was conscious now of how much Olivia knew about him. His housekeeper had turned a blind and clearly unimpressed eye to his goings-on in Paris; why she felt the need to remind him of them now, he wasn't sure. He didn't like it.

'I'll have to think of an apt comparison,' he said as he reached for her hand. Her skin was cool and soft. 'An icicle, perhaps? Glittering, perfect and rather cold.'

'That sounds more like a criticism.'

'Well…' Aziz answered with a hint of a wolfish smile. 'Icicles melt.'

Olivia melted just a little then, her fingers tightening on his, her cheeks pinking again as she looked away. Her reaction, Aziz decided, was delightful. 'Come,' he said as he drew her further into the room. 'Dinner is waiting.'

'This is all very romantic,' she murmured as she let him lead her to the table. Her fingers felt fragile and slender in his, and he let go of her hand with reluctance.

He knew, logically at least, that acting on the desire he felt for Olivia was out of the question. It would complicate what needed to be—for the sake of the monarchy, not to mention his marriage—very simple.

God willing, Olivia would be flying back to Paris tomorrow—and he would have found Elena.

Yet he still wanted to enjoy himself tonight.

As if she could read his mind, Olivia asked, 'Is there any news on Queen Elena?'

Aziz shook his head. 'I'm afraid not.'

'This Khalil wouldn't... He wouldn't hurt her, would he?' Concern shadowed Olivia's eyes and Aziz felt an answering clench of both worry and anger in the pit of his stomach.

'I don't think so. There would be no purpose to it and, as you said earlier, she is a reigning monarch. Kidnapping her is bad enough, but hurting her would have international consequences.'

'That's true,' Olivia said, frowning. 'But doesn't Khalil realise that? He could be brought before an international tribunal.'

'Kadar exists outside of such things.' Aziz gave her a bleak smile. 'At least, at the moment. My father ruled with an iron fist. The people loved him even so, because he was strong and he kept the country stable. But he did things his own way, and it means there are very few repercussions for what happens within its borders.'

'But surely someone from the Thallian government will protest?'

'If they find out.'

'You've kept it from them too?'

'From everyone, Olivia. I've had to. But I will find her.'
He placed the heavy damask napkin in her lap, just an
excuse to touch her. Her body quivered under the brush
of his fingers. 'I understand you have questions,' he continued quietly. 'But I'd much rather talk about something
else. Something pleasant, even.' He smiled, willing the
tension and uncertainty of the last few hours, the last few
weeks, away, if just for one evening.

'Something pleasant,' Olivia repeated, her long, slender fingers toying with the crystal stem of her wine glass.
Her mouth curved and she glanced up at him, eyebrows
raised. 'Nothing comes to mind at the moment, I'm
afraid.'

His lips twitched in an answering smile. 'Oh dear,'
he murmured. 'What a dilemma. Surely we can come
up with something?'

'Do you really think so?'

'I'm sure, between the two of us, we could think of
something pleasant indeed.' His voice had dropped to a
husky murmur and his insides tightened with desire. He
hadn't intended a sexual innuendo, but it was there all
the same. He heard it and, from the way Olivia moist-
ened her lips, he knew she did too. He wondered what
she would do with it, how she would respond...and how
he wanted her to.

'I'm sure you think of *something pleasant* all the time,'
she answered. 'Although, that's a euphemism I haven't
come across before.'

'Rather an innocuous one,' he answered, and her expression tightened.

'Don't flirt with me, Aziz. I know it's your default
setting but you managed to keep yourself from it before.'

He let out a laugh. 'My default setting?'

She faced him directly, her gaze now resolute. 'You're a playboy. You can't help it.'

He smiled wryly. 'You make it sound like I have some condition. A disease.'

'One I'd hope you can control. I'm not going to be one of your conquests.'

She was going on the attack because their little bout of flirting had disconcerted her, Aziz decided. Had affected her. 'Default settings aside,' he said, leaning back in his chair, 'I like seeing you smile, Olivia, and hearing you laugh. I've only heard you laugh once before, and I wasn't even in the room.'

A wary confusion clouded her eyes. 'I don't know what you're talking about.'

'You were in the kitchen and I'd come into the house without you knowing it. I heard you laugh.' He paused, noting the way her face went pale, her eyes widened. 'It was a delightful laugh,' he continued. 'Rich and full, almost dirty. I wondered what you were laughing about.'

'I—I don't remember.'

'Why don't you laugh like that with me?'

'Maybe you're not funny enough,' she shot back, on the attack again, and he nodded, smiling.

'Ah, a direct challenge. I now have a mission.'

'One you'll fail at, Aziz. I'm your housekeeper. You don't need me to laugh. You don't even know me.'

'And is there very much to know?'

Her fingers tightened around her wine glass. 'Not really. I live a very quiet life in Paris.'

'Why is that?'

'I prefer it.'

'Yes, but why?' He realised he truly did want to know the answer, wanted to understand why a woman like Olivia Ellis—a beautiful, capable, intelligent, lovely woman—would hide herself away as housekeeper to an empty house for six long years.

'Why shouldn't I?' she challenged. 'Not everyone wants to live like you do, Aziz.'

He sat back in his chair, amused and still intrigued by her non-answer. 'And how do I live, Olivia?'

'You know as well as I do. Parties till dawn and a different woman in your bed every night.'

'You disapprove.'

'It's not for me to judge, but it's certainly not how I want to live my life.'

'Surely there's a balance? We're opposites, you and I, in our pursuit of pleasure, but don't you think we could find some middle ground?'

Her eyes flashed. 'And where would that be?'

In bed. He had a sudden, vivid image of Olivia lying on top of tangled satin sheets, her glorious hair spread out on the pillow, her lips rosy and swollen from his kisses. His libido stirred insistently. He knew he had no business thinking like this, feeling like this.

And yet he did.

'It's up for discussion, I suppose,' he said easily, and Olivia just shook her head.

A waiter came in with their first course and they both remained silent as he laid plates of salad before them. Olivia kept her head bowed, her face averted, although she murmured a thank you as the man departed.

'I don't think he suspected,' Aziz murmured as the door clicked shut.

Olivia glanced up at him. 'Like you said, people believe what they want to believe.'

She sounded hard, Aziz noted, and cynical. 'Has that been your experience?'

'More or less.'

'Which one?' he asked lightly, and she stared at him, her whole body going still, her face turning blank.

'More,' she said flatly, and then looked away. He wanted to ask her what she meant but she didn't give him the chance. 'Will you miss your old life?' she asked. 'The parties, the whole playboy routine? I suppose things will be very different for you, getting married, living in Kadar.'

'Yes, I suppose they will.' He picked up his fork and toyed with a piece of lettuce. 'But in answer to your question, no, I won't miss my old life.' He glanced up, taken aback by his own honesty, striving for nonchalance. 'Which I suppose is a confession of how shallow I really am.'

She cocked her head, eyeing him thoughtfully. 'A shallow person wouldn't be fighting for his throne.'

'Maybe I just want power.'

'Why *do* you want to be Sheikh?' she asked. 'You never even seemed interested in Kadar before. You hardly ever returned here, by your own admission.'

'It isn't a question of want,' Aziz answered after a moment. 'It's my duty.'

'A duty that didn't concern you before,' she pointed out and he pretended to wince.

'You don't pull your punches, do you, Olivia?'

'Why should I?'

He chuckled softly. 'No, I don't suppose you should. It's a fair question, anyway.' One he didn't particularly want to answer, yet he felt the surprising need to be honest. So much of his life was pretence and prevarication. Olivia, with her direct gaze and no-nonsense attitude, was someone he knew he could trust and confide in, at least a little. 'My father never really wanted me to be

Sheikh,' he said after a moment. 'I was always a disappointment to him.'

'But why?'

Because he'd wanted Khalil. Even when he knew he wasn't his son, when he'd rejected him, Hashem had longed for the son he'd loved, not Aziz. Not his son by blood. Honesty only went so far, though, and Aziz wasn't about to admit any of that. He couldn't stand it if Olivia ended up pitying him and the desperate-for-love boy he'd been. 'We just didn't see eye to eye on a lot of things.' Which was putting it mildly.

Even now he could remember the way his father had sneered at his every attempt to please him. He could feel the scorching shame he'd known when Hashem had marched him into a meeting of royal aides and staff and asked him to recite Kadar's constitution. Aziz had stumbled once, *once*, and Hashem had mocked him ruthlessly before slapping his face and dismissing him from the room.

Just one memory among dozens, hundreds, all of them equally cringe-worthy. Until he'd been fifteen and he'd lost his virginity—to one of his father's mistresses, no less—and he'd realised there was another way to live. A way not to care.

'Is that why you've stayed away from Kadar? Because of your father?' Olivia asked, and Aziz blinked back the memories and stretched his lips into an easy smile.

'Pretty much. Our meetings were—acrimonious.'

'But you still haven't told me why you've chosen to return to Kadar and be Sheikh.'

'I suppose,' he said slowly, 'It's a bit of perversity on my part. I want to prove my father wrong. I want to prove I can be Sheikh, and a damned good one at that.' He heard the passionate intensity throb in his voice and felt a shaft of embarrassment. He sounded so *eager*.

'So your decision is still about your father,' she said after a moment. 'You're still letting him control you. Letting him win.'

He jerked back, stung more than he liked by her assessment, yet knowing she was right. His choices were still dictated by his father. He might not wear his heart on his sleeve any more, but he still wanted his father's approval. *His love.*

'I never thought of that before,' he said as carelessly as he could. 'But, yes, I suppose you're right. It's still about my father.' And maybe it always would be.

'It's hard,' Olivia said quietly, 'When someone has so much power and influence in your life, to let go of it. Even choosing to ignore that person still makes them the centre of your life, in a way. You're spending all your energy, all your time, trying not to think about them.'

'You're speaking from experience,' Aziz observed and she shrugged.

'Like you, I'm not very close to my father. He's still alive, of course, but we haven't spoken in years.'

'I wasn't aware of that.' He thought of her father, an easy-going, affable man who had climbed high in the diplomatic service. 'He recommended you for the position as housekeeper,' he recalled and she nodded stiffly.

'I think he felt he owed me that much, at least.'

'Owed you?'

She shook her head and he could tell she regretted saying even that much. 'It doesn't matter. Ancient history.'

But he saw how her hands tightened in her lap, her features became pinched, her eyes darkened with remembered pain, and he knew it wasn't that ancient. And it did matter.

She looked down at her plate, her expression clearing, Aziz suspected, by sheer force of will. 'Anyway, we should be talking of the future, not the past,' she said briskly. 'Assuming you find Queen Elena in time, do you think you will come to love her?'

Aziz stiffened in surprise. *No, never.* Because he wasn't interested in loving or being loved, didn't want to open himself up to those messy emotions, needless complications. Look where it had got him; you loved someone and they let you down. They didn't love you back or, worse, they hated you.

But he wasn't, thank God, a needy, foolish boy any more. He was a man who knew what he wanted, understood what he had to do, and love didn't come into it at all.

'Queen Elena and I have discussed the nature of our marriage,' he informed her. 'We are both satisfied with the arrangement.'

'That isn't really an answer,' Olivia replied, and Aziz smiled and spread his hands.

'We barely know each other, Olivia. I've met Elena twice. I have no idea if I could love her or not.' 'Not' being the operative word. 'In any case, I'd rather talk about you. I'm sure you're far more interesting than I am.'

She shook her head rather firmly. 'I most certainly am not.'

'You're the daughter of a diplomat. You must have grown up in all sorts of places.' She conceded the point with a nod and Aziz pressed, 'Where would you call home?'

'Paris.'

With a jolt he realised she meant his house. No wonder the job meant so much to her. It was probably the longest she'd lived anywhere.

'Not just because of now,' she explained. 'I spent some

time in Paris as a child—primary school years. I've always liked it there.'

'And where did you spend your teenaged years?'

The slightest hesitation. 'South America.'

'That must have been interesting.'

A tiny shrug, the flattening of her tone. 'It was a very small ex-pat community.'

Which was a strange response. She had secrets, Aziz thought. He thought of that rich laugh, the anguished piano music. She hid all her emotion, all her joy and pain—why?

Why did he hide his?

Because it hurt. It hurt to show your real self, to feel those deep emotions. They were both skimming the surface of life, he realised. They just did it in totally different ways.

'And if I recall your CV, you only spent one year in university?'

'One term,' she corrected, her voice giving nothing away. Her face had gone completely blank, like a slate wiped clean. 'I decided it wasn't for me.'

Her knuckles were white as she held her fork, her body utterly rigid. And even though he was tempted to press, to know, Aziz decided to give her a break. For now. 'I'm not sure if it was for me either,' he told her with a shrug. 'I barely scraped a two-two. Too busy partying, I suppose.'

He saw her relax, her fingers loosening on her fork. 'A playboy even then?'

He shrugged. 'It must be in my genes.' And there could be some truth to that, considering how many women his father had had. But Aziz knew that, genetics aside, his decision to pursue the playboy life had been deliberate, even if it was empty. Especially because it was empty.

'You're clever, though,' Olivia said after a moment. 'You started your own consulting business.'

'I'm fortunate that I have a way with numbers,' he said dismissively with a shrug. In truth, he was rather fiercely proud of his own business. He hadn't taken a penny from his father for it, although people assumed he had. In reality he hadn't accepted any money from his father since he'd left university. Not that he went around telling people that, or about the percentage of his earnings that he donated back to Kadar to support charities and foundations that helped women and children, the vulnerable and the oppressed. He wasn't going to brag about his accomplishments, or try to make people like him more.

Except, maybe he needed to, if he wanted to keep his throne.

'What about you, Olivia? Did you ever want to be anything other than a housekeeper?'

Her eyes flashed ire. 'There's nothing wrong with being a housekeeper.'

'Indeed not. But you're young, intelligent, with the opportunity of education and advancement. The question, I believe, is fair.' He waited, watching the play of emotions across her face: surprise. Uncertainty. Regret.

'I intended to study music,' she finally said, each word imparted with obvious reluctance. 'But, as you know, I dropped out.'

He thought again of her playing the piano, the passion and hopelessness he'd seen on her face. 'You never wanted to take it up again?'

She shook her head, decisive now. 'There was no point.'

'Why not?'

She pressed her lips together, her gaze turning distant. 'The music had gone,' she finally said. 'The desire, along with the talent. I knew I couldn't recapture it even if I tried, which I didn't want to do.' She sounded matter-of-fact but he felt her sadness like a palpable thing, like a cloak she was wearing that he'd just never seen before, never seen how it suffocated her.

For beneath that cool, remote exterior, Aziz knew there hid a beating heart bound by pain. A woman who had suffered…but what? And why?

He wanted to know but he kept himself from asking. She'd shared enough, and so had he. They both had secrets, and neither he nor Olivia wanted them brought to light. Yet he could not keep himself from wondering. He'd touched something dark and hidden in Olivia, something he shouldn't let himself feel curious about, yet he was.

He wanted to know more about this woman.

Olivia shifted in her seat, avoiding Aziz's penetrating stare, and focused on her salad. He was asking too many questions, questions that felt like scabs being picked off old wounds.

She'd put her memories in a box in her mind, sealed it shut and labelled it 'Do Not Open. Ever'. Yet with his light questions, his curious tone, Aziz was prying off the lid.

She didn't think about her dreaded term at university when she'd been like a sleepwalker, only half-alive, if that. She didn't think about her music, although she'd surrendered to the desire and even the need to play a couple of times in the last few years. Playing the piano was like a blood-letting, all the emotions and agonies streaming out along with the notes.

She'd needed the release because the rest of the time she kept herself remote, distant, from everyone and everything, even her own feelings, her own heart.

Life was simpler, and certainly safer, that way. She'd fallen apart once, overwhelmed by emotion, by grief, guilt and pain, and she had no intention of letting it happen again. If she gave those dark feelings so much as a toe-in they'd take over everything. They'd swamp her soul. And she might never come up for air again.

So she stayed numb, safe. She kept a tight rein on her emotions, let herself be content with a half-life.

Yet in the few hours since she'd been with Aziz too many of those emotions had been stirred up. Grief. Joy. Guilt. Hope. Aziz stirred up everything inside her. He asked questions, he made her smile, he touched her with his teasing in a way she hadn't expected and couldn't let herself want.

She'd thought she was dead inside but when Aziz had kissed her she'd felt gloriously, painfully alive.

Out there on the balcony she'd almost responded to his barely there kiss and turned it into something else entirely. She'd felt as if she'd been teetering on a wonderful precipice and part of her had wanted to swan-dive into that chasm of feeling and see if she really could fly.

She would have dropped like a stone. That life, a life of wanting, feeling, *loving*, was over.

'What will you do if you don't find Queen Elena in time?' Olivia asked. No more talking about herself.

'Failure is not an option.'

'And I assume Khalil feels the same way.' She didn't want to involve herself in complicated Kadaran politics, yet part of her was curious, intrigued by the sudden spike of bitterness she'd heard in Aziz's voice, the surprising darkness she'd seen in his eyes when he'd spoken of Kadar or his father—or this illegitimate son who was now trying for the throne. 'Did you ever meet him?' she asked. 'Khalil?'

Aziz smiled, but it belied the sudden coldness in his eyes. 'Yes. Once.'

'When?'

'When I was a child. He was living at the palace, and I was the pretender then.'

'You were? How?'

'I was the son of my father's mistress, an acknowledged bastard. My father legitimised me when he banished Khalil. It was not a terribly popular move, I'm afraid.' He spoke as if it didn't really matter, but Olivia knew it did. It had to.

'Is that why people support Khalil now?'

'They've always supported him. He left the country when he was seven, but he's remained in everyone's hearts—the poor little prince who got booted out. And I've always been the smug brat who took his place.' He still spoke lightly, but his eyes were like iron.

'It sounds like your father didn't think through his decision very wisely,' Olivia said quietly, and Aziz let out a laugh, the sound harsh and abrupt.

'My father,' he answered, 'Wanted to have his cake and eat it too. And he didn't even like cake.'

'So he loved Khalil,' she said slowly, 'But he still banished him.'

'I've often wondered why he did, since he made it clear what a disappointment I was compared to Khalil.' Aziz's mouth twisted in something like a smile. 'I suppose he did it because he was so angry that he'd been made a cuckold. Or maybe he was furious with himself for loving a son who wasn't actually his. Or maybe he just reacted out of anger and pain.' He took a breath and let it out slowly. 'I think he made this will because he wanted to give Khalil a chance.'

She met his gaze directly. 'A chance you don't want to give him.'

Aziz jerked back as if he'd been slapped. 'Why should I? He's not the ruler by right. *I* am.'

'But do you even like Kadar?' Olivia pressed. 'You've spent so little time here by your own choice.' She shook her head slowly, realisation dawning. 'You're only doing this to spite your father, and he's dead.'

She saw anger blaze briefly in Aziz's eyes before he gave her a rather sardonic smile. 'What an astute psychological assessment, Miss Ellis.'

'Sarcasm is the lowest form of defence.'

'I thought the expression was the lowest form of humour.'

'That too,' she conceded. 'I'm not saying you don't deserve to be Sheikh, Aziz, although—' She stopped and his gaze narrowed.

'Although…?'

'Although I wonder if you think you do,' she finished quietly.

He stared at her, breathing hard, as if he'd been running. Olivia held his gaze, wondering why she'd pushed him yet also glad that she had. 'You're right,' he finally said. 'I do wonder if I should be Sheikh. If the people don't want me to be, if my father didn't…'

'And yet you're still here.'

'When I first read my father's will I thought about just giving it up to Khalil. Turning my back. I think plenty of people were expecting me to.'

'But you didn't.'

'No, I didn't.' He spoke heavily, as if he doubted the wisdom of his choice. Doubted, Olivia suspected, himself.

'Well, I think that says something,' she said and Aziz glanced at her with a hint of his old humour.

'Oh? And what does it say? That I'm stubborn and bone-headed?'

'And determined and strong,' Olivia answered. 'Aziz, you're the Gentleman Playboy.'

'As you keep reminding me—charming, shallow, feckless and so on. Yes, I know.'

'Forget shallow and feckless for a moment,' Olivia said. 'You're charming. You have most of Europe eating out of your hand, and I don't just mean the women. Why shouldn't you be able to win the hearts of your own people? You just haven't tried before.'

He pressed his lips together as if to keep from saying something, then after a moment gave a little smile. 'Thank you for that pep talk. It was obviously needed.'

So he was reverting to lightness, Olivia thought. She was disappointed and yet she told herself it was just as well. They'd had enough emotional honesty for one evening, surely.

'Enough talk about Kadar and politics,' he said, pouring them both more wine. 'Let's talk about something else.'

'Such as?'

'What do you like to do in your spare time?'

'What?' Startled and more than a little discomfited, she simply gaped at him. Aziz smiled back, his teeth gleaming white in his tanned face, his eyes like silver. Her insides tightened in helpless, yearning response. Why had she never responded to him like this before?

Because you never let yourself. Because she'd never spent so much time with Aziz that hadn't been mundane and perfunctory. Because she'd never got to know the man behind the persona before—a man who was more thoughtful, sensitive and appealing than the Gentleman Playboy but with all of his charm and charisma.

'Hobbies, Olivia. Pastimes. Do you like to read? Go to the cinema? Crochet?'

'Crochet?'

He shrugged. 'A shot in the dark.'

An unwilling bubble of laughter escaped her, surprising her. She was enjoying this silly banter, she realised. She liked how it made her feel. 'I don't crochet, I'm afraid.'

'No need to be afraid. I'm not disappointed.' She laughed again and Aziz's eyes flared. 'There it is. That lovely sound. I will find out why you laughed in the kitchen.'

She shook her head slowly, still smiling. 'It was nothing.'

'It was a wonderful laugh.'

'I was laughing at a squirrel,' she told him. 'A little red one. He was trying to pick up a nut and it was too heavy for him.'

She'd watched that little squirrel for several minutes, had been absorbed in his little drama, and when he'd finally managed to pick up the nut she'd laughed. It had been such a silly little thing, but it had taken herself out of her own head for a little while, and she'd needed that.

'No big mystery,' she told Aziz lightly and he smiled.

'But now you intrigue me even more. You make me wonder why I've never been able to make you laugh before, yet now I can.' He held her gaze then, still smiling, but with a certain steadiness in his eyes that made Olivia's mouth dry—for wasn't this far more dangerous, this emotional connection, than a merely physical one?

A man who could make her laugh as well as burn.

She looked away.

'Olivia?' Aziz said quietly.

'I suppose laughter doesn't come easily to me any

more,' she said after a moment. She was amazed she was telling him this much, yet part of her wanted to tell him, to unburden herself, if only just a little.

'Why is that?'

She just shrugged. She didn't want to unburden herself that much, to admit that she'd thought the carefree, laughing girl she'd once been had died when she'd been just seventeen and it had felt like her soul had been ripped from her body. It *had*.

Aziz reached over and placed his hand gently on top of hers. 'Whatever has made you sad,' he said quietly, 'I'm glad to see you happy, even if just for a moment.'

She nodded jerkily, her throat so tight she knew she couldn't manage any words even if she'd known what ones to say.

Aziz removed his hand and sat back. 'Are you finished?' he asked, gesturing to her half-eaten salad. 'I'll call for the next course.'

Olivia nodded, grateful for the reprieve from their conversation, and a few minutes later the waiter returned to clear their plates and then bring the main course. Aziz asked for some mundane details about the Paris house, and by silent agreement they kept the conversation about various issues concerning the house and nothing else for the rest of the meal.

Yet, even though Aziz wasn't asking her personal questions any more, Olivia couldn't keep her mind from wandering to places it shouldn't go. She couldn't keep her gaze from roving surreptitiously over him, or from noticing the way the candlelight gave his hair a blue-black sheen.

He wore an evening suit that emphasised the breadth of his shoulders, the trimness of his hips, the overall perfection of his body.

Everything about him was graceful and elegant; Olivia was mesmerised just by the way he held his knife and fork. He had lovely fingers, she thought: long and slender, yet with so much latent strength. There was, she decided, a leashed and stealthy power about him that she hadn't noticed before, at least not consciously. Perhaps now that he was ruler of a country she felt it, had the sense that he was more than a man of wealth and charm.

A dangerous man.

A desirable man.

And that was something she had no business thinking about. Aziz was getting *married.* Determinedly she yanked her gaze away from those long-fingered hands. He was getting married in just two days, if he found Queen Elena.

And if he didn't?

Not her problem. Not a question she needed to answer, or even ask. Yet her heart lurched all the same.

The candles had burned down to waxy stubs by the time they had their coffee, thick and syrupy, brewed in the Arabic manner that made Olivia pucker her mouth.

Aziz laughed when he saw her expression. 'It does take some getting used to.'

'You're obviously used to it,' she said, for he'd drunk his without so much as a grimace, or even adding any sugar.

'It took a while,' he admitted as he finished the last of his coffee. 'But the taste of it has grown on me.'

'So you don't miss your Americanos?' Olivia asked with a little smile. She'd made his coffee on the machine he'd had installed in the kitchen of the house in Paris.

'Oh, I miss them,' Aziz assured her. 'But I've made a point of having only Kadaran food and drink since I've been here.'

'To show your loyalty?'

'Something like that,' Aziz agreed, and Olivia sensed the brush-off. He was, she realised, constantly playing himself down. She thought suddenly of what Malik had said: *there are more loyal to Aziz than he knows, or allows himself to believe.* She thought she understood a little of what the older man had been saying; she'd felt it from Aziz tonight.

He didn't believe in himself. He didn't believe he would be accepted by the Kadaran people *as* himself. And maybe his careless, playboy attitude was just a cover-up for the fear and doubt he felt inside.

Or was she being fanciful because she knew how much she hid herself? This was *Aziz*, after all, the darling of Europe, a confident, charismatic man who had women constantly fawning over him. How could he possibly doubt *anything*?

Yet she wanted to know, wanted to know who the real Aziz was, and that was a foolish, dangerous thing to want, because he affected her too much already, and in any case he wasn't hers to know.

With effort she swallowed her questions down. She didn't need to know more about this man. She couldn't allow herself to, or let the attraction that had leapt to life today turn into something even deeper and more powerful, something she hadn't even thought she was capable of any more.

No, it needed to end here and now. Tomorrow she would be back in Paris and Aziz, hopefully, would have found Queen Elena.

She rose from the table and gave him a cool smile. 'Thank you for dinner.'

Aziz arched an eyebrow, and just that one little quirk made her feel sure he knew what she was doing and why. That he knew she was afraid and attracted all at once, but of course the Gentleman Playboy would never say so.

'Thank you for humouring me and continuing this charade,' he answered, rising also. He stepped closer to her and her heart seemed to stutter. She was achingly conscious of his nearness, even the smell of him, a citrusy aftershave that she must have smelled a thousand times before but now made her feel dizzy with longing. She knew she should move back and yet she didn't. She couldn't.

Aziz dipped his head and his gaze seemed to heat her from within, kindling feelings and needs that she'd thought were no more than cold ash. 'I'm sorry to have put you to such trouble, but you were the first person I thought of, Olivia. The first person I knew I could trust.'

The sincerity in his voice made the flames inside her rise higher. Logically she knew this had to be mere flattery. She was his housekeeper, for heaven's sake, and of a house he only visited on occasion, one step up from a maid—and he *trusted* her? *She* was the person he'd first thought of in a time of trouble?

Yet the warmth of his gaze and the seeming sincerity of his tone caused a maelstrom to whirl inside her. Desire and something deeper, something fiercer—the longing to be needed, to be important to someone again, to *matter*.

Ridiculous.

She barely knew Aziz. And this whole thing, on both their parts, had been nothing more than an act. Everything that had happened between them had been fake.

Even if it didn't feel fake.

'I'm glad to have been of service,' she said crisply and took a step away from him. The gauzy skirt of her dress caught on the stiletto heel she wasn't used to wearing and she tripped backwards, her arms windmilling as she desperately attempted to right herself, even as she braced herself to land on her backside.

Aziz stepped forward in one fluid movement and caught her in his arms. He brought her body into close, exquisite contact with his. She felt their hips and thighs collide and desire shot through her as if she'd been injected intravenously with lust. It sizzled through her whole body, pulsed between her thighs. She let out a ragged gasp and Aziz's gaze darkened, came to rest on her parted lips.

Olivia could only wait. Her heart had started a heavy, insistent thud and, despite her resolutions of a mere moment ago, her whole body yearned and strained for him to kiss her, to feel so much, even more than she already had. *So much more*.

For a second, no more, she thought he might kiss her. He leaned forward, drawing her body even closer to his so she felt the hard press of his arousal, and that electric pulse of want jolted her yet again, right down to her toes.

Then he stepped back, steadying her, and dropped his hands. She swallowed, fought for composure and tried to arrange her expression into something neutral and bland, as if the whole world hadn't tilted on its axis and all her certainties hadn't scattered. As if she hadn't suddenly realised how stark, dull and empty her life had been and how she now wanted so much more.

Wanted Aziz.

Aziz smiled but now it seemed like a mere stretching of his lips. His eyes, Olivia saw, were dark and fathomless.

'Thank you,' she muttered and Aziz nodded in acknowledgement. 'I should— It's late.' She stopped, took a breath and let it out slowly. 'Goodnight,' she said, the single world coming out with far too much finality.

'Goodnight, Olivia,' he said softly, and with a jerky nod, lifting her dress up so she wouldn't trip again, Olivia hurried from the room.

CHAPTER FIVE

AZIZ GAZED GRIMLY at the dawn sky. The sun was a huge, orange ball peeking above the horizon, spreading its morning rays over the courtyard, bathing the palace in brilliant, golden light.

His mood, however, was as dark as a moonless night. He'd spent most of the night awake, surveying satellite printouts of Kadar's desert, searching for a possible camp-site for Khalil and his band of rebels. From a satellite it was possible to discern various settlements, but neither Aziz nor any of his aides had been able to determine whether such settlements contained Khalil—or Queen Elena.

He'd sent another troop of soldiers, the few he felt he could trust, to investigate the most promising settlement which, when compared with printouts from the last few weeks, had shown the most activity. But it was three hundred miles from Siyad and the men were going by Jeep, as a helicopter would surely alert Khalil…if he was even there.

And if he *was* there? How far would his once-believed half-brother go to gain the throne? Would he risk his life and, more importantly, would he risk Elena's?

Aziz had told Olivia that he didn't think Khalil would be so foolhardy, but the truth was he didn't know. He didn't know Khalil at all.

He had, since taking the throne, read all the information the Kadaran intelligence service possessed about him. Khalil had been banished, along with his mother, at the age of seven, and his aunt had taken him to live with her in America. He'd gone to an elite boarding school and university, worked in business for a while before serving in the French Foreign Legion for seven years.

Aziz suspected it was while in the army that Khalil had made the contacts that had enabled him to return to Kadar. To return to the people who had wanted him back, had embraced him. The people of Siyad might like having a cosmopolitan man with European ways and a head for numbers as their ruler, but the heart of Kadar, its desert tribes, wanted Khalil. And it was the heart Aziz was concerned about.

Once more you're trying to win someone's heart, he thought cynically. *Trying to make someone love you. When will you realise you can't? You never will.*

Except he hadn't even started trying, because he was afraid he'd fail.

Olivia had been amazingly astute about it all. Her observations still stung him hours later. She'd seen how he still wanted to please his father, knew that he was afraid to try. How had she seen so much? How had he revealed it?

It was incredibly unsettling, to be understood in that way, yet there was something strangely, intrinsically good about it too—because Olivia hadn't rejected or judged him because of his fears. She'd encouraged him by insisting he could win the Kadaran people to his side…if he just tried.

The trouble was, he didn't think he believed her. From behind him Aziz heard the door softly open and close.

He glanced over his shoulder and saw Malik standing to attention, waiting for his order.

Malik had been on his father's staff, had known him as a boy. He knew how Aziz had been sneered at and mocked by his father and most of the palace staff. He'd stepped in more than once to deflect his father's contempt and, even though Aziz was grateful, he also felt the squirming shame of having his weaknesses exposed in front of another person.

'We're no closer to finding Elena, are we?' he said, a statement rather than a question.

'On the contrary, Your Highness, the settlement we viewed earlier on the satellite photograph looks promising. There has been an extraordinary amount of movement to and from it, as you saw, and just now we were able to find a photograph from the day Queen Elena was taken. It shows several vehicles on the outskirts of the camp.'

Aziz swivelled in his chair. 'That is promising, Malik,' he said. 'But, even if the soldiers I deployed enter the camp and Queen Elena is there, there is no guarantee as to what might happen.'

'No, indeed, Your Highness.'

Aziz sighed wearily and raked his hands through his hair. 'Can I even blame Khalil?' he said, only half-asking. Sometimes he felt furious at Khalil for endangering not just his bride, but his whole country. Did the man he'd once thought was his half-brother actually *want* war? Would that be his revenge for Sheikh Hashem's rejection of him?

Yet for seven years Khalil had believed himself to be his father's son, his country's heir. And he must know that Aziz had stayed away from Kadar for years; maybe he assumed Aziz didn't want to be Sheikh.

Maybe he believed he'd be a better one.

'It's my father I really blame,' Aziz told Malik. 'For making marriage a condition of my rule. For not naming a successor and inciting dissent with this damned referendum.' He shook his head, fury and despair warring within him. 'He was trying to create instability. He wanted it both ways.'

'You don't know that, Your Highness.'

'Don't I?' Aziz turned to give Malik a shrewd, bleak look. 'You know, Malik, that he never wanted me as his heir. He never—' He swallowed down the pathetic words 'loved me' and said instead, his voice rough, 'Really accepted me as his son.'

'But you are his son. His only son. And those in Siyad, and in the palace, know that. They believe you are the rightful ruler.'

'But many others don't. Many wonder if Khalil was treated unfairly. If my father banished him simply because he'd grown tired of his mother and preferred mine.'

'They will learn the truth.'

'Will they? Or will my entire rule, however long it even is, be dogged by such rumours?' He turned to stare out of the window; the courtyard was now shimmered in the morning heat. 'Damn my father,' he said in a low voice. 'Damn him to hell.'

'Perhaps he is already there,' Malik answered quietly.

'I'm not normally quite this negative, am I?' Aziz said, smiling at his aide, the action both false and familiar. *Smile. Laugh. Joke. Act like you don't car, and then maybe you won't.*

It didn't seem to fool Malik, however, for the older man gave a small, sorrowful smile and inclined his head. 'Your sentiment is understandable, Your Highness. Much of this current trial is your father's doing, I know. But there are more loyal to you than you realise.'

'I can't gamble on the people's loyalty, Malik. Not when I've been away for so long.' Aziz shook his head. 'I have two days to find Elena,' he stated. 'Two days before the six weeks are up and I lose my throne.'

'You have men looking for Elena, Your Highness,' Malik said. 'There is no more you can do now. They should have a report back to you by tonight.'

'Which gives me one day to make an alternative plan.'

'Speaking of alternative plans...' Malik cleared his throat. 'You are meant to attend the opening of the Royal Gardens in Siyad's city centre with Queen Elena today.'

Aziz closed his eyes. 'Damn it, I forgot. Can I cancel?'

'It's not advisable.'

'I'll go alone, then.'

Malik hesitated. 'Again, not advisable. Yesterday's appearance on the balcony was very popular.'

'You mean they want to see Elena again.' *Olivia.* Malik nodded. 'I don't think she can pull it off, Malik—even if she agrees, which she won't.'

'She could be veiled.'

'Veiled? Siyad is more modern than that.'

'It would be a nod to tradition, a way to show the more conservative parts of the population that you and your queen will respect the old ways.'

'Even if I want to change them?'

'Respect can exist with change.'

'I don't know.' He didn't like the thought of yet more pretence. More lies.

'Her eyes would be visible,' he said at last.

'Coloured contact lenses,' Malik answered swiftly.

Aziz shook his head slowly. 'It's too dangerous. They might ask her to speak.'

'Nothing beyond a murmured pleasantry, probably in Arabic.'

'I doubt Olivia knows any Arabic.'

'She can learn a few phrases.'

'It's madness.' Aziz rose abruptly from his chair and strode to the window, bracing one hand against the ancient stone arch. '*Madness*. What happens if they find Elena at the camp? How do I explain that?'

'You don't. We fly her in discreetly and have her replace Miss Ellis, who returns to Paris as she wished, no one the wiser. It's the ideal outcome, Your Highness.'

'And what if we don't have the ideal outcome?' Aziz queried grimly. 'What if we can't find Elena, or we find her and she's hurt, or—' He swallowed down the words, the awful possibility he did not want to give voice to. Fury towards Khalil surged inside him. Damn the man who had made his life hell, even when he'd been thousands of miles away. 'What then?' he demanded of Malik. 'How do we explain the fact that I've been posing with my bride for the last two days?'

'Not easily,' Malik acknowledged. 'But we've already taken this risk by having you appear on the balcony. It was a gamble, Your Highness, even a desperate one, but necessary. You know that.'

Yes, he knew that. He knew how unstable and insecure his reign really was. How one more whisper could start a firestorm of doubt and rumour that would ravage his entire kingdom…or even start a civil war.

'I'll go speak to her,' he said, and turned from the room.

Olivia lay in the massive bed, staring up at the silk canopy above her. Morning light filtered through the slats of the shutters Mada had drawn over the windows last night. It couldn't be much past dawn, and already the room was hot, the air still.

Today she'd return to Paris, to familiarity and safety. She felt a wave of relief mixed with a treacherous flicker of disappointment.

She didn't want to leave. She'd enjoyed herself with Aziz, enjoyed the attention and interest of a gorgeous, sexy man whose touch made her whole body tingle. A man who made her laugh, made her wonder, made her *feel*.

After so many years of numbness she knew now that some contrary part of her yearned for more from her life. From Aziz. She longed for his attention, his teasing, banter and sense of fun—and for his kiss. For that rush of sensation that had fired up her whole body, had made her senses sing.

Trying to banish the desire that rushed through her just at the memory of Aziz's lips on hers, Olivia threw off the covers just as a knock sounded on the door. 'Come in,' she called, and then froze in shock when the door swung open and Aziz stepped into the room.

They stared at each other wordlessly for a long, suspended moment. Olivia was suddenly, horribly conscious that she was wearing nothing but a frothy nightgown of lace and silk that ended mid-thigh; Mada and Abra had given it to her last night. Her hair was tousled about her shoulders and she'd frozen, half-risen from the bed, so the nightgown rode up on her thighs and low on her breasts. She glanced at the nightgown's matching robe laid out on a chair a few metres away. Would it be better to grab it and put it on, flimsy as it was, or to dive beneath the covers again?

She watched Aziz's gaze rove slowly over her, saw

his eyes flare and then darken with desire. Felt her body tingle treacherously in response.

'I thought…' Her voice came out in a croak and she tried again. 'I thought you were one of the women who had helped me last night.' She glanced at the clock and saw it was only a little past seven. 'Has something happened?'

'As much as I would enjoy discussing such matters with you in this moment, I fear I would be far too distracted.' His gaze dipped meaningfully to her scanty nightgown, his mouth curving into a teasing smile. 'Perhaps you could meet me for breakfast?'

Olivia felt a prickly flush spread over her whole body, even as a pleasure at his little bit of flattery stole through her. She'd distract him? She liked the sound of that… even if she shouldn't.

'Yes, of course,' she managed, willing her body-blush to fade.

'I'll send the women to you,' he said and with a last wicked smile he withdrew from the room.

Quickly Olivia rose from the bed and stripped off the nightgown, flinging it into a corner of the room before hurrying to the shower. Why had Mada and Abra given her such a ridiculously frothy, *sexy* thing to wear? It occurred to her then that the clothes she'd been wearing might belong to Queen Elena. Perhaps Aziz had bought them for her. Maybe that frothy nightgown was meant for their wedding night.

She blanched at the thought, hating that such a thought made her feel jealous. This was nothing more than pretend. Aziz was getting *married*, she reminded herself yet again.

Pretend or not, she knew she'd enjoyed herself more, *lived* more, in the last twenty-four hours than she had in ten years. And, even though she knew nothing could happen with Aziz, she didn't want this time with him to come to an end.

By the time she got out of the shower, Mada and Abra were waiting in the bedroom with a fresh set of clothes. Olivia tried to explain to them that she wanted her old clothes back, but they didn't understand and kept insisting she wear the sky-blue silk dress they'd brought.

With a sigh of defeat Olivia acquiesced; the dress was simple and elegant, belted at the waist and swirling about her knees. Pearl earrings and a necklace, along with a pair of low suede pumps, completed the outfit. Mada did her hair in a coil low on her neck, and Olivia felt a jolt of surprise as she looked in the mirror. She still wasn't used to her dark hair.

'Thank you,' she murmured, and the two women smiled and nodded, clearly pleased with their effort.

Malik was waiting outside her bedroom when she opened the door. 'Good morning, Miss Ellis. May I escort you to Sheikh Aziz?'

She nodded and followed him through the maze of the palace to a pleasant room at the back. The French windows were thrown open and a table had been set for two on a private terrace overlooking the palace gardens. Aziz rose from the table as she approached.

'I hope you don't mind eating outside. It's early enough not to be hot.'

'It's lovely,' she said. The air felt fresh and the view of the terraced gardens, lush and green, even though Siyad was in the middle of a desert, was beautiful.

'Coffee?' Aziz asked with a glinting smile as he proffered the little brass pot.

Olivia gave a little grimace. 'I admire your tenacity in getting used to it. I suppose I should do the same.'

Too late she realised that she'd made it sound as if she intended to stay in Kadar. She reached for her napkin and laid it in her lap. 'Are the pilot and plane ready to return me to Paris?'

'Yes, as soon as you are.'

Again she felt that mingled rush of relief and disappointment. 'Good. Thank you.'

'It is I who should be thanking you,' Aziz answered. 'You have helped me immeasurably, Olivia.'

There was something about the way he said her name that made her insides shiver. She suppressed the reaction and took a sip of the strong coffee. 'Is there any further news of Queen Elena?'

Aziz put down his coffee cup, his narrowed gaze on the horizon. 'We've had some progress. My men are investigating a desert settlement that has had some unusual activity, according to satellite photographs. I'll know by tonight if Elena is being kept there.'

'I hope she's found.'

'As do I.' Aziz turned to look at her; there was something so solemn and steady about his grey gaze that Olivia stilled. The Gentleman Playboy looked awfully serious, but then she knew now there was more to him than what he showed to the world.

'What is it?' she asked, because even though he hadn't said anything she felt there was something.

'I have no right to ask anything more of you, Olivia,' Aziz said. 'But I am a desperate man in desperate circumstances.'

Nothing about Aziz, Olivia thought, seemed desperate. From the moment she'd met him he'd been powerful, confident, assured. So much so that she still had trouble believing he could ever doubt himself. 'What do you want?' she asked, although she had a feeling she already knew.

'To stay one more day. I'm meant to open the Royal Gardens in the city centre with Queen Elena this afternoon. They've been redesigned. It would be no more than cutting a ribbon—'

'Cutting a ribbon?' Olivia shook her head in disbelief, even though happiness rippled through her at his request and at the realisation that she might be able to stay longer. 'It would be a lot more than that, Aziz. I'd have to talk to people, stand right next to them… I wouldn't fool anyone for a minute, or even a second.'

'That was my concern as well,' Aziz replied easily. 'But you'd be veiled and wearing traditional Arabic dress. It's not necessary in Siyad, but it would be seen as a sign of respect for the old ways, and happily it would be convenient for us. The only thing people would see of you is your eyes.'

'And my eyes,' Olivia pointed out, 'Are blue. I don't know what colour Queen Elena's eyes are, but I'm quite sure they're not blue.'

'They're grey. And we could use coloured contact lenses.'

'Coloured—' She stopped abruptly and shook her head. This was getting too deep, too dangerous, even if part of her wanted to stay. To be with Aziz. That, she thought darkly, was even more dangerous than any masquerade. 'No, I can't. I'm sorry. It's too risky.'

'You think I'm not aware of the risks?' Aziz answered, one eyebrow arched. He spoke casually enough but she felt the suppressed tension and even anger in him.

Olivia sat back, still shaking her head. 'You must be, of course,' she said slowly.

'I have far more to lose than you do, Olivia,' he told her quietly. 'Surely you see that. Even if we were discovered, your part in this plot would be easily explained and dismissed. You're my employee, after all. I could have coerced you, or threatened you with dismissal.'

'But you wouldn't!'

'Of course not!' He shook his head, smiling, yet clearly a bit affronted. 'What kind of man do you think I am?'

'I don't know what kind of man you are, Aziz,' Olivia answered, although she certainly felt she knew him better now than she had twenty-four hours ago—and she knew he was not the kind to blackmail or threaten. She knew him better than she knew anyone else in her life, which was a sad commentary on how isolated she'd been. Even so, she made herself state, 'I barely know you.'

'You've been in my employ for six years.'

'And in all that time I've seen you only a few times a year, for a few minutes at a time, to discuss the house or your social calendar. I don't *know* you.'

She stared at him; her words seemed to echo through the room, taking on a new, deeper meaning.

Aziz stared back at her, his eyes glittering like gun metal. 'I think you know me well enough to know I would never mistreat you or anyone,' he said, and his voice once again held that wry lightness Olivia now suspected hid other, darker emotions. Hurt or anger or even despair.

'I don't think you would mistreat anyone,' Olivia told him quietly. 'And I don't think you'll fire me if I refuse to continue with this charade.'

'No, I won't. Your job is secure, Olivia, if that's what you're really worried about.' He paused, watching her thoughtfully for a moment. Olivia tried not to squirm under that silvery gaze. No, she wasn't just worried about her job. She was worried about her heart. Her soul.

'All I'm asking for is a favour,' Aziz resumed. 'And, yes, I know it is a big one. Come to the Royal Gardens with me today and you can fly home to Paris tonight.'

He made it sound so simple. And it felt so tempting. To be someone else for a day, to *feel* like someone else, light, happy and free...

Desired.

Olivia gazed out at the stunning view and tried to resist. 'And what will you do if Queen Elena isn't found?' she asked after a pause. 'Tomorrow is meant to be your wedding day, Aziz.'

She looked up to see him do a mock double-take. 'Wait, *tomorrow*?' She gave a small, answering smile as his smile turned bleak. 'I have to find her, Olivia. And I will.'

'But if you don't,' Olivia pressed, even she knew she shouldn't—shouldn't ask, shouldn't know, shouldn't care. 'What will you do? The six weeks run out tomorrow.'

'I'll have to think of something else.' Aziz met her gaze directly. 'But that is not your concern, Olivia. All you need to do is accompany me to the gardens today.'

'Couldn't you just say Queen Elena is indisposed, or tired?'

He shook his head. 'Our appearance on the balcony yesterday was very popular, and things are unstable enough as it is. If people found out she is missing...'

'Why hasn't Khalil said anything?' Olivia asked suddenly. 'Surely he knows how dangerous the situation is, just as you do? Why hasn't he admitted he has Queen Elena?'

'Because even in Kadar kidnapping is illegal,' Aziz answered with a grim smile. 'And Khalil is gambling that I won't want people to know she is missing.'

'And he's right.'

'Yes.'

'Couldn't you talk to Khalil? Reason with him?'

'Possibly, if I could reach him. At the moment he

doesn't want to be found. In any case, I'm not sure either of us is in the right frame of mind for a nice chat.'

Aziz turned away to gaze once more out at the garden; Olivia could hear the tinkling of a fountain in the distance. 'I know this is a risk, Olivia,' he said quietly, his gaze still on the gardens. 'But it is my risk, not yours, and one I must take—not just for duty's sake, but because I need to.' He turned to her, his gaze grim, yet blazing.

'And not just for the sake of my country but for the sake of my own soul. You told me I was insisting on claiming my title because of my father, and you were right. Part of my desire to return to Kadar is bound up in that. But a bigger part is about reclaiming my country's past. Healing it, and healing my own soul.' The smile he gave her seemed sad. 'I spent my entire childhood feeling inferior. I want to prove to myself as well as my people that my father was wrong. That I can be a good ruler.' His smile turned wry, mocking. 'And now you can cue the triumphant violins. Find a handkerchief to dab the tears from your eyes.'

'I'm not teary,' Olivia told him, although she actually was, a little. She'd heard such sincerity, such raw honesty, in Aziz's voice. 'But I understand, Aziz. Maybe more than you even realise.'

Wasn't her own soul at stake too? Aziz was bringing her back to life, painful as that was. Maybe, when she returned to Paris, she'd be strong and alive enough again to want; to feel; to try, just as he was trying.

They were helping each other, in a strange and totally unexpected way.

Aziz nodded slowly. 'If you choose to return to Paris today, I will respect your decision.'

He waited, silent and still, for her answer. An answer,

Olivia knew, that she should give immediately and un-equivocally.

No. Of course not. This dangerous charade had gone on long enough. She owed Aziz nothing, no matter what she felt for him now. And it was too dangerous to stay here, to spend time with him. Dangerous in a way that had nothing to do with impersonating Queen Elena…and all to do with her contrary, alive-again heart.

'Well?' Aziz asked softly.

Olivia didn't speak. She stared at Aziz, saw a faint smile curve his lips, yet his eyes, those lovely, grey eyes, were filled with a sorrow that cut right to her heart.

She drew a breath and let it fill her lungs. She shaped her mouth to form the words, *'No. I'm sorry, Aziz, but I can't'.*

They filled her head, echoed through her, yet the ones that came out of her mouth were different.

'All right, Aziz,' she heard herself say. 'I'll do it.'

CHAPTER SIX

OLIVIA STARED AT her reflection in a kind of incredulous wonder. If she'd thought she looked different with dark hair, she looked like an utter and complete stranger in the Arabic dress Abra and Mada had put her in. Unfamiliar grey eyes stared back at her in the mirror from above a black gauzy veil that covered her nose and mouth. A *hijab* hid most of her hair, save for a bit peeking out on her forehead, and her figure was swathed in a voluminous Arabic dress of grey shot through with silver thread.

She could not imagine elegant Queen Elena wearing such a get-up, but she supposed she would have had to, if she were here.

Instead, Olivia was wearing it. And, even though she'd agreed to this, she still felt disbelieving that it was actually happening.

She'd felt a kind of dazed incredulity all morning, from the moment she'd told Aziz she'd do it. The smile he'd given her had been dazzling, melting the last of her inhibitions even as she'd tried to caution herself. Aziz might have woken up feelings inside her, but those feelings didn't have to be about him. For him.

Yet so many of them were. She *liked* this man, more than she'd ever expected to. And she was poised to feel a whole lot more, if she let herself.

Which she wouldn't.

The rest of the morning had been given over to getting her ready: touching up her hair, putting in the coloured contact lenses that made her eyes itch, donning these clothes. Turning herself into a stranger. Yet she'd agreed to it because she wanted to help Aziz.

Because she wanted to be with him. She didn't just like him; she liked being with him. She liked who she was when she was with him. She felt, amazingly, more like herself. Like the girl she used to be: lighter; happier. More hopeful, and when she'd thought hope had long passed her by.

Don't you realise how dangerous this is?

A knock sounded on the door of her room and then Malik appeared. 'Miss Ellis.' His dark gaze swept over her and he nodded in approval. 'Well done.'

'I don't think anyone would be recognisable under all this,' Olivia said and Malik's normally stern face cracked into a small smile.

'And that is good for us. Are you ready?'

'I suppose.'

'Sheikh Aziz would like to go over the particulars of the afternoon with you before you depart. I'll take you to him.'

Olivia's robe whispered along the floor as she followed Malik out of her bedroom. She felt so strange, as if she were wearing a costume for a fancy-dress party. She half-expected someone to come up to her and rip the veil away from her face, laughing that she hadn't fooled anyone.

'Sheikh Aziz,' Malik announced, opened a set of double doors and ushered Olivia into an elegant salon. He closed the doors behind him, leaving her alone with Aziz who she saw was also wearing traditional robes and a turban.

'The dark hair and high heels suited you,' Aziz said after a moment. 'And, amazingly, so does this ensemble.' He smiled, his eyes crinkling at the corners, his good humour utterly infectious so that Olivia smiled back, even though she knew he couldn't see it beneath her veil.

'Should this be my new housekeeper's uniform, do you think?'

'I'll think about it,' Aziz replied thoughtfully, and Olivia's smile widened.

'I feel rather ridiculous.'

'You look lovely, even so. I wonder, how can a woman still look beautiful when she is completely covered?'

'You tell me.'

He walked towards her, his gaze sweeping slowly over her. 'You are beautiful, Olivia. You are very beautiful.' He smiled, his eyes glinting, inviting her to share his good humour. 'I should be comparing you to flower petals, I suppose.'

She let out a little gurgle of laughter. 'Now, that would be a bit stale. I think you need to find some new flattery, Aziz.'

'Is it flattery if it's the truth?'

Pleasure flared deep inside. The truth was, she did feel like a flower, like something once dormant and dry that had finally found sunlight, sought water. 'That's not saying much,' she bantered back. 'Considering I've changed my hair and eye colour and am currently covered from head to toe.'

'True. I must admit, I prefer you in the evening gown you wore last night.'

Another flare of pleasure, deeper, fiercer.

She nodded towards his own robes, a turban covering most of his dark hair. 'And is your outfit part of this plan to show respect?'

'Indeed, yes.' Wryly he glanced down at his *thobe*. 'This get-up is just about as strange to me as yours is to you.'

'You look good. You should wear it more often,' she teased, half-amazed at herself, at the humour and happiness Aziz brought out in her, even in the midst of all that was going on. Aziz smiled back, his eyes sparkling.

'Maybe I'll surprise you.'

You already do. Aziz's devotion to his country, his determination to rule, hinted at depths she'd never even guessed at. He was a man she'd thought careless, judged as shallow. And yet, to her surprise, the light, laughing man known as a playboy enchanted her now as much as the deeper, more thoughtful man she was beginning to realise hid underneath. She liked laughing with him, teasing and being gently teased, especially when she now knew there was more to him than his charming façade.

'So what now?' she asked. 'When are we meant to appear at the gardens?'

'In a short while.' He smiled and took a step towards her. 'But first I need to teach you a few phrases in Arabic.'

'Arabic?' Olivia stared at him in alarm. 'Why?'

'Because the people will expect it, and it will please them to hear you speaking their language.'

'Except I can't speak their language,' Olivia pointed out, unable to keep a high note of panic from entering her voice.

'No one will expect you to speak it well, or even understand what you are saying,' Aziz assured her. 'Elena had learned a few phrases only.'

'Which is a few more than I've learned.'

His mouth curved in the kind of smile that invited her to share the joke. Jump right into it. 'Hence, our lesson,' he said, his voice nearly a purr, and then he took her by the hand, causing those sparks to race up her arm, and drew her towards him. 'Come.'

He led her to a private alcove with a velvet divan and, sitting down, he drew her by the hand so she sat next to him, the folds of her robe spilling over his own. She could see the outline of his powerful thigh beneath the fabric that had drawn taut when he'd sat down, inches from her own leg. She was mesmerised by the sight of his leg; she couldn't stop staring at it. It was if her brain had slowed down; everything in her focused on Aziz and this incredible, unbearable awareness of him.

Why hadn't she felt like this when she'd sat with him in the drawing room of the Paris house, going over accounts?

Because she hadn't been truly alive then. Aziz hadn't woken her up, made her want.

Want him.

She drew a shaky breath and smoothed her robe over her lap, just to give her hands something to do. She forced her gaze upwards, away from his thigh. His eyes were dancing. 'So; Arabic. What do I need to say?'

'Let's start with hello: *"assalam alaykum".*' His voice, as soft and rich as velvet, caressed the syllables of the unfamiliar words, making them sound as if they were an endearment, even though Olivia knew he was only saying hello. *Hello.* Her body didn't seem to grasp that fact.

'Olivia?' He raised his eyebrows, expectant, and she realised she'd just been gawping at him, her brain and body both on overload from the simple presence, the sheer masculinity, of him.

'*Assalam alaykum,*' she repeated, fighting a flush, half-afraid that Aziz would be able to guess the nature of her thoughts. Surely he could see her body's reaction to him? She felt as if everything in her both tingled and ached, and she was afraid she might not be able to control the overwhelming need to touch him. What would he do if she did touch him? If she just reached out and stroked his face, or touched that taut and powerful thigh? *Squeezed it...*

'Let's try it again, shall we?' Aziz murmured, his smile seeming to wind around her heart, which thumped harder.

'I'm nervous,' she muttered, and he nodded.

'It's understandable.'

Except that she wasn't nervous for the reason he thought: the upcoming appearance; the charade. She was nervous because of him: because of his nearness and this all-consuming attraction that was getting so very hard to fight. Because of these feelings and desires that were flowing up and out of her, impossible to ignore or resist.

'Assalam akaylum,' he said again and she forced herself to repeat it as best as she could. Aziz gave a little nod. 'Good. Now this one is a little longer.' He smiled, his gaze warm and encouraging. *'Motasharefatun bema refatek.'*

Olivia's eyes widened. *'Motashar*—what?'

Aziz laughed softly, the sound no more than a breath. 'I know, I know, it's a mouthful. Try again.' He said the words again, and Olivia did her best to repeat them. 'Good. One more time.' She did and he smiled and nodded, reaching over to squeeze her knee covered by the heavy gown.

Olivia felt as if she'd been branded. She lurched upright, sparks zinging through her system, making her feel more agonisingly alive—all because he'd touched her knee.

Aziz glanced down at his fingers, still wrapped around

her knee. 'Sorry,' he murmured but he didn't sound at all repentant. 'I guess I got carried away.'

He was teasing her, Olivia knew. He was a playboy, after all, hidden depths or not. How many women had he taken to bed? How many had he kissed? He probably didn't even remember their names, and here she was, quivering because he'd touched her knee through a thick robe. He must think she was pathetic. Her desire for him must be horribly, humiliatingly obvious.

'What does it mean?' she managed, and was thankful her voice came out sounding normal—almost.

'"Pleased to meet you".' Aziz paused and Olivia braced herself for him to say something embarrassing, like *I know this is difficult, when you're so obviously attracted to me.* Not, she acknowledged, that Aziz would ever say such a thing. She didn't think he'd ever intentionally humiliate her. But the knowledge she saw in his eyes was bad enough. The moment passed and he just smiled and asked, 'Shall we try it again?'

Olivia nodded.

They went through a few more Arabic phrases, no more than pleasantries that Aziz assured her she wouldn't be expected to say faultlessly—which was a good thing, because she was still having trouble concentrating on anything at all.

'Did you speak Arabic growing up?' Olivia asked when they'd finished. 'Is that why you're so good at it?' Her head was buzzing from all the words she was afraid she wouldn't remember, and also from this impossible awareness of Aziz. During their little lesson her heart rate, thankfully, had begun to slow, and it had been easier to breathe. Now, however, she felt everything kick into overdrive for he'd moved closer to her and his thigh nudged hers.

'Yes, I spoke it as a child.' He smiled, but she saw that hardness enter his eyes, and sadly she wondered whether he had a single happy memory from his childhood.

'But you didn't speak it much as an adult, did you?' she asked. 'In Europe?'

He shrugged. 'Not often. But I think you always remember the language of your childhood.'

'Well, I'm still impressed,' Olivia told him. 'I'm rubbish at languages, always have been. Perhaps you could tell?'

His eyes gleamed with amusement—and maybe something else as well. 'Not at all.'

'Every time we moved somewhere new, my father tried to get me to learn the language,' Olivia continued. 'But I was hopeless, no matter how hard I tried.'

'You seem like someone who always does the best she can.'

Except she hadn't done the best, not when it had mattered the most. She'd been too afraid, too hurt, too weak. Her throat went tight and she shook her head, not wanting to say any more, wondering why she'd said as much as she had.

She kept *saying* things to Aziz, things she'd kept to herself for so long, and even though it scared her part of her actually wanted to say them. Wanted someone to understand her in a way she'd never let herself be understood.

And more than that: she wanted not just to be understood, but to be resurrected. To be the laughing, carefree girl of her youth; to have her innocence. To be the girl she'd thought dead and buried, whom Aziz had called back to life.

And maybe that was his gift to her, giving her that desire. Even when they reverted back to their usual roles when she left Kadar, perhaps she could still be thankful that he'd woken her up.

Except she knew waking up meant feeling everything: not just the joy and lightness but the darkness, the despair. The feeling that you weren't whole, that you were sleepwalking through life, soulless and empty...

'Olivia?' Aziz took her by the shoulders and gave her a gentle shake. 'Where did you go?'

She blinked up at him, the memories receding, even though that awful feeling of emptiness remained. 'I'm right here.'

Aziz frowned. 'For a few seconds there you looked as if you were lost in your memories, and they weren't good ones.'

Somehow she managed to summon a smile. 'I'm okay,' she said, which was no answer at all, and wasn't even true.

Aziz stared at her for a long moment, his hands still on her shoulders. Olivia stared up at him, and even with the emptiness echoing inside her she felt her heart start to thud, her bones start to melt. She didn't want him ever to let her go, and for a heart-stopping second she thought he might actually draw her closer, whether for a kiss or just a hug. In that moment it didn't even matter; she just wanted him to touch her.

A knock sounded at the door and slowly, reluctantly, Aziz released her. Olivia sat back against the divan, her heart still thudding so hard she thought Aziz might be able to hear it.

'Enter,' he called, and Malik came into the room.

'Your Highness, the car is ready.'

'Thank you, Malik.' Aziz turned to Olivia with his usual charmingly wry smile, the intensity of the previous moment seemingly completely forgotten, though its aftershocks still rippled through her. 'Your chariot awaits, madam.'

Smiling back, trying to stuff all the feelings and memories back down inside, Olivia rose from the divan and followed Aziz from the room.

A dark sedan with tinted windows was waiting in the palace courtyard. The gates were closed, but spectators still lined the other side of the fence, and when they emerged from the palace a cheer went up that nearly sent Olivia reeling backwards.

Aziz steadied her with a firm hand on her lower back. 'The crowd already loves you.'

Olivia gave a shaky laugh. 'You mean they love Queen Elena.'

'How could they,' he murmured, dipping his head low so his breath fanned her cheek, 'When she's not even here?'

'It's the idea of her,' Olivia answered as she slid into the car, arranging the voluminous folds of the robe around her. 'The idea of your bride. I suppose,' she mused, 'It doesn't really matter who it is.'

She'd just been thinking aloud, but from the sudden stillness, the arrested look on Aziz's face, Olivia felt as if she'd said something momentous. 'What is it?' she asked warily, but Aziz just shook his head.

'Nothing. Nothing at all.'

It doesn't really matter who it is.

The words echoed through him. *It doesn't really matter... It doesn't really matter... It doesn't really matter who it is...*

All he needed was a bride, a willing wife. Elena had been suitable, certainly, but she wasn't here now. And, if he couldn't find her, she wasn't suitable at all.

But Olivia was.

Part of Aziz was appalled at how quickly he was willing to discard one bride for another; another part of him was amazed he hadn't thought of it before.

He had two days. Olivia was here. Suddenly it seemed simple.

Of course, Aziz knew it wasn't really remotely simple. He was considering marriage and, while it had been expedient for both him and Elena, it certainly wasn't for Olivia. She had no reason, and perhaps no desire, to marry him.

He glanced at her; the headdress and veil were hiding most of her face. Her grey eyes and Arabic clothing might make her look like a stranger but he saw something familiar in the curve of her cheek, the fullness of her lips.

Lips he'd touched and tasted...

There was an attraction between them, even if she wanted to deny it, as well as a friendship, or at least the beginnings of one. Surely both were a good basis for marriage? At least for the kind of marriage he wanted: one without any emotional risk.

And he suspected Olivia might want that kind of marriage too.

Maybe it could work.

'Aziz?' Olivia was peering out of the window and nibbling her lip. 'Look.'

He looked and saw that the narrow streets of the Old Town were lined with people. Distantly he registered the roar of the crowd. The people were throwing flowers onto the car. He watched a single blood-red rose hit the window and fall to the ground.

His people loved his bride.

His fake bride. The bride they thought was Queen Elena of Thallia, not a nobody, a housekeeper from Paris.

What the hell was he going to do?

'We're very popular,' he said lightly, giving Olivia a reassuring smile. Her face had gone pale.

'This could all go horribly wrong,' she said, her voice low, her gaze still on the crowds outside the window. The car had slowed to a crawl.

'Not for you,' Aziz answered. 'Only for me.'

'You know I'd be affected.' She leaned back against the seat and closed her eyes. 'I must have been mad to agree to this. *Mad.*'

Aziz gazed at her, wanting to reassure her but knowing he couldn't, at least not now. They were in the car; she was dressed as Queen Elena. Calling a halt to the charade now would be disastrous to them both.

'I'm sorry,' he said suddenly, and she opened her eyes and looked at him. He held her gaze; it felt as if they were somehow connected.

'Thank you for saying that,' she said quietly. Her mouth quirked into a tiny, teasing smile. 'Even if there's nothing you can do about it.'

'Too true.' He nodded towards the street; they'd left the Old Town and were entering the central square of Siyad's more modern district. The square was filled with people too, all of them proffering bouquets and gifts. Crowds and flowers. 'Those people aren't just going to go away.'

'No, I don't suppose they are.'

He leaned over and touched her hand, wanting the contact, needing it, and suspecting she needed it too. 'You'll be fine, Olivia. You'll be wonderful. You're elegant, lovely and gracious, and you're warm and friendly when you let yourself relax.'

'Was that your pep talk?' she answered with raised eyebrows, but she was smiling. 'How am I supposed to relax in front of about a thousand people?'

'If anyone can do it, you can.' He squeezed her fingers before withdrawing his hand. 'We're here.' The car had pulled up in front of the main gates to the public gardens and several security personnel jumped out of the car in front and cleared a path to their door. Aziz took a breath and gave Olivia a reassuring smile. 'Are you ready?'

'As ready as I'll ever be,' Olivia said with an attempt at flippancy that almost worked. Aziz felt a swell of admiration for this woman whom he was coming to realise was courageous, not just capable. She was strong, sweet and incredibly, amazingly, sexy.

'That's my girl,' he murmured and she looked away, trying to hide her smile.

One of his staff opened the door. 'Let's go,' Aziz said and, taking her hand, he helped her out of the car.

CHAPTER SEVEN

FLASHBULBS BLINDED OLIVIA for a moment and flowers fell
at her feet, causing her to stumble as she exited the car

Then Aziz slid his hand around her waist, steadying her, and she felt her confidence come back. Someone spoke to her in Arabic, an incomprehensible babble,
and Aziz murmured in her ear. 'Steady, now. *Assalam
alaykum.*'

'Assalam alaykum,' she repeated, and managed to
force her lips into something like a smile, even though
she realised belatedly that no one could see it behind her
veil. *'Assalam alaykum.'* There. That sounded slightly
more natural. And the people around her obviously understood what she meant, because their smiles grew
wider and another cheer went up.

Olivia kept smiling and nodding; her head felt light
and her heart was beating so hard it felt as if it would
jump right out of her chest. Aziz stepped slightly away
from her and she felt the loss. She needed his strength
now. She needed *him*.

He spoke to someone else in Arabic and an old woman,
her face almost completely hidden by her veil, reached
for Olivia's hand and patted it, murmuring something in
Arabic. Olivia felt tears spring to her eyes.

She was touched, humbled and ashamed all at once.

She felt like such a fraud. She wanted this to be real. Her emotions rose like a tidal wave inside her, drowning out practical thought, capable action.

From somewhere she found the unfamiliar words. *'Motasharefatun bema refatek.'* She mangled the phrase but the woman understood and beamed. Aziz slid a sideways smile at her, his eyes so warm with approval that Olivia blushed.

Then he took her hand and led her through the crowd to the gates of the Royal Gardens. A red silk ribbon ran across them; someone handed Aziz a rather wicked-looking knife. He made some joke about it in Arabic, for several people laughed and nodded. Then he raised the knife high over his head and slashed the ribbon in two. Everyone cheered. Olivia clapped her hands and smiled at the people around her, who beamed back.

They wanted to like her, she realised, just as they wanted to like Aziz. How could he not see that? How could he not see that his people were ready and waiting to accept him?

Because he doesn't accept himself.

Someone spoke to her in Arabic, smiling and gesturing to her veil, which Olivia guessed had met with people's approval. They wanted to see Aziz's bride, but appreciated the sign of respect for the old ways, as Aziz had said they would.

She smiled wryly back and patted her hijab, trying to convey how strange and yet acceptable it was to wear it. Somehow this actually worked, for the woman she was talking to clapped her hands and crowed with laughter.

Olivia felt something unfurl in her soul. *Hope.* Happiness. She'd cut herself off for so long, she'd actually forgotten how much she missed being with people. Besides talking to workmen and the concierge across the

street, she'd lived the last six years in virtual isolation—
and by choice.

Maybe now she would finally have the strength to
choose differently. Maybe that would be Aziz's legacy
to her, his gift.

Finally Aziz reached for her hand and drew her towards
the garden. They stepped through the gate and it closed
behind them, leaving them blissfully alone in an oasis
of beauty and scent.

'Is no one coming in with us?' Olivia whispered and
Aziz smiled and shook his head.

'No, this is our private time. As a couple.'

'Oh. Well, that's a relief, I suppose.'

'I think you fooled them.'

Olivia bit her lip, remembering the way the old woman
had smiled at her and touched her hand. 'I feel like such
a fraud. Like a liar.'

Aziz was silent for a moment, his gaze on the brick
walkway in front of them. 'I know,' he said finally. 'I
do too.'

'You shouldn't,' she said impulsively. 'You're not pretending to be someone else.'

'Aren't I?'

She shook her head. 'I think you believe you are somehow, but your interest is genuine, Aziz. I can tell. So can
they. You may not see it, but the people want to accept
you. To love you.'

His mouth twisted. 'The people of Siyad, maybe. And
only because they think I'm sophisticated and glamorous.'

'Well,' she answered, daring to tease, 'You *are* sophisticated and glamorous. You're the Gentleman Playboy, after all.'

'On the surface, maybe. That's not who I really am.'

She stopped walking and nearly stopped breathing. 'Then who are you, Aziz? Really?'

He paused mid-stride and for a moment she thought he'd say something real, something important. Then he turned to her with a teasing smile. 'Well, I'm not answering that question until you answer it too.'

'What do you mean?'

'You can't tell me *you're* an open book, Olivia. You're hiding something.'

'Not hiding,' she answered stiltedly, unnerved by his perception. 'Just—not thinking of it. Why dwell on bad memories?'

'Why indeed? I'm in a beautiful garden with a beautiful woman.' His eyes glinted teasingly. 'What should I compare you to? Not rose petals, since you've heard that one before.'

'You'll think of something, I'm sure,' Olivia answered.

'Just give me a moment.' He strolled down the path, his hands behind his back. 'In any case, I actually mean it, Olivia. You don't act as if you know it or believe it, but you really are a beautiful woman.'

'Is that another line?' Olivia answered back, unnerved by the sincerity in his voice, and he turned to face her, all levity and artifice gone from his face.

'No, it's not.'

He looked so serious, so *intent*. Olivia's mouth dried and her mind spun. She licked her lips and shook her head. 'Aziz…' She didn't know how to articulate what she felt, all the hope and fear. She loved being with him, loved his attention and interest, but she was also afraid. Being woken up to all these feelings was scary. It meant you could get those same feelings hurt.

'Just a simple statement of fact,' Aziz said with a smile. 'I can't help but notice.'

'Always charming,' Olivia answered, half-teasing, glad to retreat back to banter. 'No wonder you're called the Gentleman Playboy.'

'Such a silly nickname.'

'How did you come to get it, then?'

He studied a crimson flower intently while Olivia waited. 'One of the gossip magazines gave me the nickname a few years ago and it stuck.'

'Why did they give you it?'

'Because they interviewed one of my former lovers and she said I'd been a gentleman throughout our relationship.' He spoke matter-of-factly but Olivia still flushed. *One of my former lovers.* Images, provocative and craven images, danced through her head.

'And what did she mean, you'd been a gentleman?'

He turned to her with a gently mocking smile. 'So curious, Olivia.'

'Maybe I am,' she answered boldly. 'Maybe I can't understand how "gentleman" and "playboy" go together.'

'It's simple. Just choose women who don't want anything from you but sex.' As he spoke his voice hardened. He turned away, leaving Olivia even more curious.

'Isn't that all you've wanted?' she asked after a moment. It certainly seemed as if it had been, judging from his many casual affairs she'd witnessed over the years.

'Yes, of course it is. How could I ever want anything more?' There was something mocking and bitter about his words, his voice, and Olivia didn't understand it. By his own admission he'd chosen his lifestyle; he didn't want serious relationships... Yet in that moment she wondered if at least part of him did.

YOUR PARTICIPATION IS REQUESTED!

Dear Reader,

Since you are a lover of our books – we would like to get to know you!

Inside you will find a short Reader's Survey. Sharing your answers with us will help our editorial staff understand who you are and what activities you enjoy.

To thank you for your participation, we would like to send you 2 books and 2 gifts – **ABSOLUTELY FREE!**

Enjoy your gifts with our appreciation,

Pam Powers

**SEE INSIDE
FOR READER'S
SURVEY**

For Your Reading Pleasure...

FREE!

We'll send you 2 books and 2 gifts
ABSOLUTELY FREE
just for completing our Reader's Survey!

YOUR READER'S SU[...]
"THANK YOU" FREE GIFTS [...]

▶ **2 FREE books**

▶ **2 lovely surprise gifts**

PLEASE **FILL IN THE CIRCLES COMPLETELY TO RESPOND**

1) What type of fiction books do you enjoy reading? (Check all that apply)
- ○ Suspense/Thrillers   ○ Action/Adventure   ○ Modern-day Romances
- ○ Historical Romance   ○ Humour   ○ Paranormal Romance

2) What attracted you most to the last fiction book you purchased on impulse?
- ○ The Title   ○ The Cover   ○ The Author   ○ The Story

3) What is usually the greatest influencer when you <u>plan</u> to buy a book?
- ○ Advertising   ○ Referral   ○ Book Review

4) How often do you access the internet?
- ○ Daily   ○ Weekly   ○ Monthly   ○ Rarely or never

5) How many NEW paperback fiction novels have you purchased in the past 3 months?
- ○ 0 - 2   ○ 3 - 6   ○ 7 or more

YES! I have completed the Reader's Survey. Please send me

the 2 FREE books and 2 FREE gifts (gifts are worth about $10) for which I qualify. I understand that I am under no obligation to purchase any books, as explained on the back of this card.

❑ **I prefer the regular-print edition**
106/306 HDL GGA4

❑ **I prefer the larger-print edition**
176/376 HDL GGA4

FIRST NAME   LAST NAME

ADDRESS

APT.#   CITY

STATE/PROV.   ZIP/POSTAL CODE

EMAIL

HP-914-SUR-13

BUSINESS REPLY MAIL
FIRST-CLASS MAIL   PERMIT NO. 717   BUFFALO, NY

POSTAGE WILL BE PAID BY ADDRESSEE

HARLEQUIN READER SERVICE
PO BOX 1867
BUFFALO NY 14240-9952

NO POSTAGE
NECESSARY
IF MAILED
IN THE
UNITED STATES

Just as part of her did—that awake, alive part of her that was now clamouring for more.

'We should look at these flowers,' Aziz said, his good humour clearly and purposefully restored. He tugged her along by the hand. 'I'll have to say something about them when we leave the garden.'

That moment of intensity broken, Olivia gazed round at the unfamiliar shrubs and blooms. The placards indicating what everything was were in both English and Arabic, and she stepped closer to read one.

'This is certainly beautiful,' she said, indicating a deep red, overblown rose. 'How do you say "beautiful" in Arabic?'

'Jameel,' Aziz said quietly, and when she turned she saw he was staring right at her, with the same intent look as before, only more so. There was more heat in his gaze. More obvious, unashamed desire.

Her heart started to thud. Her body swayed. She wanted him to kiss her, wanted it so badly her body shook. She wondered, distantly, if he could see how she trembled.

'Let's walk,' Aziz said, his voice thick. Taking her by the elbow, he led her along the twisting walkways, vibrant blooms and bushes on either side of them.

Another intense moment had been thankfully broken, but Olivia couldn't keep the ache of want from pulsing insistently through her.

'What will you do as Sheikh?' she asked when they were deep in the heart of the garden, the sounds of the city having long faded away. Time to be sensible and have a normal conversation. 'I mean, what do you want to do? What do you hope to accomplish?'

'That's a good question.' Aziz walked alongside her for a few moments, his contemplative gaze on the path in front of them. 'I told you before that I wanted to be a good ruler—an honest and fair one.' He glanced up at her with a wry smile that also seemed a little vulnerable. 'Which is ridiculous, I know, considering the lie I've ensnared us both in now when I've barely started my rule.'

Olivia didn't reply. She might not like the charade she'd got involved in, but she understood now how Aziz had been driven to it. And who was she, really, to talk about secrets and lies? She'd been harbouring both for ten years. 'I understand why you've done what you did,' she said. 'Desperate times call for desperate measures, I suppose.'

'Yes, I suppose they do. But I hope I'll be able to put all this behind me. I want to bring Kadar into the twenty-first century in so many ways.' She heard a raw note of passion and purpose enter his voice, fuelling it. 'I want to give women more rights and I want to nationalise healthcare and bring more international business and trade to Siyad.' He let out a rueful laugh. 'And now I'm really sounding ridiculous.'

'No, you're not. Those are all admirable things.'

'And how do you suppose I will accomplish them?' Aziz stopped and stared up at the hard, blue sky. 'The people might never accept me as Sheikh.'

'You say that, but I don't see why they wouldn't, in time. They certainly loved you out there.' She swept an arm back towards the garden gates.

'They loved the idea of my marriage, which might not even happen. I'm supposed to marry tomorrow and I'm no closer to finding Elena.'

She put her hands on her hips. 'What do you want, Aziz? Do you want people to fall at your feet? Work with what you have. Go out to the desert tribes and visit them. Talk to them. You can do it.' She stepped closer to him and heard the raw passion in her own voice. 'You already are doing it, even if you don't realise it. You were natural out there with everyone, chatting and laughing and listening. People like your sincerity, not that you're some sophisticated playboy. The people of Siyad want a leader who listens and the people of the desert will want it too.'

He turned to look at her, almost seeming surprised by her impassioned speech. Olivia realised she had sounded rather fierce, but that was because she believed what she'd said. She believed in Aziz.

'You sound like my school matron, back when I was sent to boarding school when I was seven,' he said ruefully. 'She told me to stop snivelling too.'

'I didn't tell you to stop snivelling,' Olivia protested.

'No, you didn't. You said some very nice things, Olivia, and I thank you for them.'

'It wasn't just flattery. I meant it.'

For a moment he looked truly touched and at a loss for words. Olivia felt her throat close up with answering emotion. Aziz nodded once. 'Thank you,' he said simply.

They walked for a little longer, listening to the birds twittering in the trees above them, the silence between them companionable rather than tense .

'So, your turn,' Aziz finally said. 'You gave me a another pep talk. I can give you one.'

'I don't need one.'

'Don't you?' He turned to her with far too much perception in his silvery gaze. 'Why have you hidden yourself away for so long, Olivia? What sadness is tying you to the past so you feel you can't have a future?'

'It's not like that,' she began feebly and he shook his head.

'Why else would a lovely young woman like you hide herself in an empty house, tidying rooms that hardly anyone ever sees? That's not what you want to do with your life, Olivia. It's not who you want to be.'

'You don't know anything about it,' she began, and Aziz took a step towards her, his expression suddenly fierce.

'Then tell me.'

'We were talking about you.'

'And now we're talking about you. Why do you hide from life, Olivia? What happened to make you so afraid?'

'I'm not afraid,' she protested. 'It's just…easier this way.'

'Why?'

She took a deep breath, let it out slowly. 'I lost someone,' she finally said, and her voice sounded strange and distant. 'Someone who was incredibly—incredibly—' She stopped, her throat so tight she couldn't get any more words out. She *never* talked about Daniel. 'Important to me,' she finally managed. 'And when you lose someone like that… Well, it keeps you from trying ever again. It keeps you from feeling like you could try, even if you wanted to.'

She couldn't look at Aziz, not without crying, which was something she had absolutely no intention of doing. But she could feel him looking at her, felt his hand skim her cheek, slide under her veil. 'Did you love him very much?' he asked quietly, and she knew he thought she was talking about a man. A lover.

'I loved him more than life itself,' she answered, because to say anything else would be a betrayal of Daniel and she'd already betrayed him once. She wouldn't again. 'I still love him and I always will.'

Aziz's fingers lingered against her face and Olivia resisted the urge to lean into his hand, to take comfort from his caress. 'I'm sorry for your loss,' he said, and Olivia managed a trembling smile.

'It was a long time ago.'

'Even so.' His hand was still on her face and Olivia risked a glance upwards. The sympathy and kindness she saw in his eyes felt like a blow to the chest, to the heart.

'Aziz,' she whispered, although she didn't know why she'd said his name, what she was asking him for.

But Aziz must have, for his eyes darkened and his hand tightened against her cheek as he lowered her veil and brushed his thumb over her lower lip. He took a step closer to her so she could feel the heat of his body, could inhale the dizzying scent of his aftershave.

'Olivia…' he said softly, and the way he said her name made those newly wakened parts of her surge and ache. *Demand.*

And then somehow—Olivia didn't know who moved first—he was kissing her. She was kissing him. And it felt incredibly tender, wonderfully sweet, finally to be touching him as she'd wanted to for what felt like for ever. To have him touch her.

His lips moved over hers and her nails dug into his shoulders as she pressed closer to him. Sweetness gave way to urgency, a sudden, overwhelming need clawing its way out of her.

'Olivia,' Aziz said again, muttering her name against his mouth as his hands roved over her body, pulling at the shapeless robe, his fingers seeking the curves hidden underneath the heavy fabric. His tongue slid into her mouth, sweeping its softness, and Olivia moaned.

Aziz's touch was like a drug; she was instantly addicted, immediately craving more and more of him. She *needed* him with an urgency that was shocking and total.

He brought his hands up to frame her face, pulling the

hijab completely away as his fingers tangled in her hair. Pins fell on the walkway with a tinkling clatter and still Aziz kissed her, each kiss acting as a brand on her soul, ensuring she would never, ever forget this. Forget him.

He'd changed her, affected her in a way no one else ever had. He'd reached deep inside her with his laughter, his understanding and his kiss.

Oh, his kiss...

She slid her hands under his *thobe*, felt the heat of his skin through the thin linen of his shirt and pressed closer. Somehow Aziz had managed to get his hand through the front opening of her robe and he brushed his thumb over the peak of her breast, causing Olivia to let out a sharp gasp of wonder and surprise.

The noise startled them both; Aziz yanked his hand away from her and stepped back quickly, a look of appalled realisation coming over his face that might have been comical in any other situation.

As it was, Olivia felt suddenly, cringingly conscious of her undone hair, her disordered robes and fallen *hijab*, her swollen lips. Of the hunger inside her that now roared to life, demanding satisfaction.

She stared at Aziz, too incredulous about what had just happened even to be embarrassed—yet. Reality was rushing in to fill all the aching, empty places inside her, reminding her that this man was about to marry someone else; that she hadn't kissed anyone in over a decade; that what she'd just done was beyond stupid.

Somehow she managed a shaky, ragged laugh. 'Well. If anyone had seen that, they would have been convinced of your fairy-tale wedding, I'm sure.' She turned then, because she didn't trust the expression on her face, and she didn't want to see Aziz's pity. Had she kissed him first? He'd responded, but maybe only because that was what a *Gentleman Playboy* did if a woman threw herself at him. Is that what she'd done? So much for staying cool, calm, remote and *safe*.

'Olivia…'

'I need to do something about my hair.' Her voice trembled and she put shaking hands up to her head as she blinked hard.

'Let me help.' Aziz knelt on the path and began to pick up her hairpins. Olivia smoothed her robes and picked up her *hijab*. Anything to keep herself occupied. She prayed Aziz wouldn't see how her hands shook. How affected she was.

'Here.' Gently Aziz took her hair in his hands and began to rearrange it into a neat coil.

It felt almost as intimate as their kiss, to have him standing behind her, his breath fanning the nape of her neck, as he arranged her hair. She stayed still, her body taut with tension yet still aching with desire, an impossible combination, as he carefully replaced all the pins, sliding them through her hair with a slow gentleness that was nearly her undoing. He wrapped the hijab around her head and adjusted her veil.

'There. I think you're presentable.'

She kept her head bowed, still unable to look at him. 'What if people guess?'

'They'll be pleased. Like you said, it's all part of the fairy tale.' She tried to move away but he stayed her, his hands on her shoulders. 'Olivia.'

'What?' Her voice came out high and strained.

'I didn't mean for that to happen.'

So she *had* kissed him first. She closed her eyes, fought the tidal wave of humiliation and hurt that threatened to overwhelm her. 'Neither did I, as it happens.'

He laughed softly, no more than a breath of sound. 'I know you didn't.'

He *did*? She opened her eyes. His hands were still on her shoulders, his body still so close to hers. He dipped his head so his lips nearly grazed her cheek. 'That wasn't for show,' he said quietly. 'No one was watching. That was just me kissing you, Olivia, because I wanted to. Because, for a moment, it felt as if I had no choice. As if I *had* to kiss you.'

Just as she had had to kiss him. She should have felt gratified by his admission, but she only felt confused. Scared. This couldn't go anywhere, at least anywhere good. Caring for Aziz, letting him in at all, would just end in her being hurt.

'Clearly you have poor impulse control,' she said, her voice thankfully tart, and she slipped from his loose embrace. He let her go. She kept her back to him, fussing with her appearance, even though she knew she looked as put together as she was ever going to, at least without a hairbrush or mirror. 'How did you get so adept at styling a woman's hair?'

'Experience, of course,' he answered, and his voice was light again. The intimacy of the moment had been broken and Olivia was both glad and ridiculously, helplessly disappointed.

'We should go back,' Aziz said. He twitched her veil better into place, his expression shuttered. 'They will be waiting for us.'

Wordlessly, Olivia followed him through the gardens. The stillness and silence felt oppressive now, rather than peaceful, the tension tautening between her and Aziz. The gates loomed before them and with them the crowds. Olivia knew that once they entered the melee she wouldn't be able to talk to Aziz. And tonight she would leave for Paris.

Yet what could she say to him? She didn't know what had happened back in the garden; who had kissed whom or why. She didn't know how tenderness had kindled so quickly into the kind of raw, urgent passion she hadn't felt in years, decades—if ever. She didn't even know if she wanted to feel it, if she wanted to give into that kind of hunger even as her body insisted that she did.

So she said nothing.

They moved through the crowds and she mumbled the Arabic phrases Aziz had taught her, keeping her eyes lowered, her face hidden.

He helped her into the car and then they were speeding back towards the palace, still not having exchanged a word since they'd left the garden.

She snuck a glance at Aziz and saw he was looking out of the window, his eyes narrowed, his arm braced on the window frame, his fingers pressed against his temple. He looked, Olivia thought, as if he had the weight of the world on his shoulders, or at least of a country.

'Perhaps there will be news of Queen Elena when we return,' she said and, seemingly startled out of a reverie, Aziz glanced at her.

'Yes,' he said tonelessly. 'Perhaps.'

He hadn't meant to kiss her. Guilt churned sourly inside him as they headed for the palace. He hadn't meant to kiss her, Aziz acknowledged, but the kiss itself had been surprising. *Amazing.* What at first had seemed like it was going to be no more than a brush or buss had turned into something deeper and fiercer, something more *real*, than he'd ever felt before.

He might have had many lovers, plenty of mutually

satisfying experiences in the bedroom, but that was all they'd been: experiences. Not relationships, not even emotional connections. Just the soulless, pleasurable joining of bodies—which was what he'd always wanted. What he'd chosen. Anything else brought with it the possibility of pain.

Yet when he'd kissed Olivia in the garden he'd felt something different, something deeper, and for a moment he'd wanted the kind of life, the kind of love, he'd never let himself have before. .

But love had no place in any relationship he chose, any marriage. Not the marriage he'd intended with Elena, and not the one he now contemplated with Olivia.

The sedan pulled into the palace courtyard and the security personnel jumped out of the other car and opened the doors. Aziz helped Olivia out of the car while his mind buzzed with possibilities.

Tomorrow was his wedding day. *But with which bride?*

They gave one last wave for the crowds lining the courtyard and then headed into the palace.

As they walked together, Aziz noted that Olivia seemed to have recovered her composure. In the garden he'd seen how shaken she'd been by their kiss—and how desperately determined she'd been not to show him.

'Perhaps a cup of tea after you've changed? I do have English tea here.' He spoke as if their meeting would be no more than a farewell, knowing he needed to handle their next conversation carefully. Olivia hesitated and he knew she was torn between wanting to spend time with him and wanting to stay safe.

Just as he was torn. They were very similar; he was realising that more and more. Both of them safeguarded their hearts. Hid their true selves, their deepest desires. They just went about it in completely different ways.

'Very well,' she said, and after she left Aziz headed for his study where he knew Malik was waiting to debrief him.

'Well?' he asked as he strode into the room. He yanked off his turban and ran his hands through his hair. 'Any news?'

'I'm afraid not. She was at the camp, but everyone had gone by the time your men arrived.'

'Gone? Did they have warning that someone was coming?'

'It is hard to say. I suspect Khalil has gone to one of the tribes for shelter. They will hide him.'

'I know that.' Aziz pressed a fist to his temple; his head had started to throb. 'How can he command the loyalty of people he has never even met before?' he demanded, and Malik shrugged.

'He represents something to them, perhaps. The old ways, from before Hashem showed disrespect for tradition and banished a wife to take another.'

'Even though his first wife was unfaithful,' Aziz answered. He heard the bitterness in his tone but could not keep himself from it. He did not have it in him to feel sorry for Khalil or his mother, not after everything he and his own mother had endured as their replacements.

He sighed wearily and dropped his hand. 'So now Khalil has taken Elena to some other desert camp and we start all over again.'

'He can't have gone very far.'

'He could be anywhere, as far as we're concerned. We're running out of time, Malik.' Aziz swung away to stare at the window. 'My wedding is tomorrow. The six weeks are up then. If I have not married, referendum or not, this country will descend into chaos and civil war.

I will not be able to prevent it. The people's loyalties are too divided.'

'You have Siyad, Your Highness.'

'But nowhere else.' Determination hardened his heart. He would not, he acknowledged starkly, find Elena before the six weeks were up. He could not allow Khalil to put forth his claim to the throne and he was not willing to call the referendum. Whether he won or not, a civil war could still ensue, causing rebellion, insurgency and unrest.

'I must marry,' he said aloud.

'We could still find her.'

'No. It will be too late.' He turned around and gave Malik a grim smile. 'Time has run out, Malik. I must marry, and I will do so tomorrow.'

'But—'

'You know it is true.'

He was going to have to convince Olivia to marry him, whether by charm, reason or perhaps even the coercion she'd been worried about. His heart and soul rebelled against the idea, but his will prevailed. He smiled bleakly at Malik. 'My bride, after all, is right here.'

Olivia donned her plain white cotton blouse and dark trousers with a rush of relief, feeling as if she were re-assembling herself, equipping herself with a kind or armour and banishing the memory of Aziz's kiss and the restless desire it had stirred up inside her.

She was going back to Paris. Yet she knew she couldn't go back to the person she'd been, that cold, lifeless husk of a human being. She didn't even want to, not after being with Aziz. After talking to him, laughing with him.

Kissing him.

The memory of that incredible kiss, impossible to suppress, made her heart beat harder. She closed her eyes, tried once more to exorcise the feel of Aziz's lips on hers, the memory of the urgent need that had spiralled inside her, spiralled out of control so hard and fast. Another few minutes and who knew what would have happened?

She took a deep breath and willed her heart rate to slow. Whatever might have happened *hadn't*. They'd stopped, and tonight she'd return to Paris.

And, even though she couldn't go back to her old life, or lack of it, she could still find comfort in the safe routines of keeping Aziz's house. She could start slowly, perhaps, in wanting more for herself—take a class, try to make some friends; nothing too big or too scary.

The thought depressed rather than encouraged her. She didn't want to learn photography or make a new pal. In that moment, she only wanted Aziz.

She shoved the thought away as she put her hair in its usual clip and, with one last resolutely satisfied glance at her reflection, headed out of her room to find Aziz. She'd get their last meeting over with and move on, whether her heart wanted to or not.

A member of staff directed her to a suite in another wing. Two sofas faced each other and a silver tea tray had been set between them. Olivia was just debating whether she should pour when a door to an adjoining room opened and Aziz strode into the room, dressed in faded jeans and a button-down shirt that had yet to be buttoned. A towel was slung round his shoulders and his hair was wet and spiky.

Olivia felt her body stiffen, her eyes pop. She could not draw her gaze away from the tantalising glimpse of bare flesh his open shirt provided. His skin was bronze, the muscles of his chest taut and defined—Michelangelo's *David*, indeed.

'Sorry,' Aziz said, 'I didn't realise you'd arrived.' He tossed the towel onto a chair and began to button up his shirt—leisurely, Olivia thought. She forced her gaze upwards.

'I just came in. When is the plane scheduled to leave?'

'That depends,' Aziz answered. He went over to the tea tray and began to pour. Olivia remained where she stood, an unease caused by too many different feelings creeping through her. 'Here.' Smiling, his eyes silver in the afternoon light, he handed her a cup of fragrant tea. 'Milk, no sugar, yes?'

'Yes... Depends on what, Aziz?' She took the cup and sat down across from him, sipping the tea without really tasting it. Her sense of unease deepened, settled in her bones.

'Depends on the conversation we're about to have,' Aziz answered as he took a sip of his own tea.

Olivia put her cup down with a clatter. 'You want me to stay longer, don't you? What is it now— another appearance? A dinner?' She spoke accusingly, but she couldn't deny the anticipation, the excitement, she felt at the thought of staying. Of being with Aziz for longer.

'No. I don't want you to pretend to be Queen Elena again. Ever.'

The finality of his tone made her head spin, her mouth gape. 'What, then?'

'I want you to be yourself, Olivia,' Aziz continued steadily. 'I want you to stay here as Olivia, not as Elena.'

'Why?'

'Because,' Aziz answered, 'I want to marry you.'

CHAPTER EIGHT

'DON'T FAINT,' AZIZ SAID, laughter lacing his voice, and Olivia shook her head as if to clear it. The dizziness still spiralled inside her, along with a thousand feelings. Shock. Hope. Fear. *Joy.*

'I'm not going to faint,' she said, and her voice sounded strange to her own ears. 'I just can't believe you said what you said.'

'That I want to marry you?'

'Yes.'

'Well, I do.'

Still she just stared, shock making speech or even thought virtually impossible. Finally she found the sense to string some words together. 'What about Queen Elena?'

'She's not here.'

'You're *engaged* to her, Aziz. Doesn't that mean anything to you?'

The lightness left his face and his eyes and voice both turned steely. 'Of course it does. But we became engaged because it was convenient for both of us. I have accepted the fact that I am not going to find her before the six weeks set out in my father's will are up. Therefore I must find another bride.'

'And you suppose I'll do.'

'I think,' Aziz said, his voice dropping to a knowing murmur, 'Based on the kiss we shared earlier today, you'll more than just do, Olivia. There's an attraction between us—'

'That doesn't mean I want to get *married*.' Olivia swung away, her whole body trembling with the shock of Aziz's proposal. Although, she acknowledged as she swallowed a near-hysterical laugh, he hadn't actually *asked*. He'd just told her his intention.

'I can't believe you'd actually suggest such a thing,' she muttered. 'It's crazy.'

'I'll admit, this whole situation has an element of madness to it. But needs must.'

'For you.' Olivia turned around, her body trembling, this time with indignation and even hurt. 'Needs must for *you*, Aziz. But I have no need to get married. Unless— unless you're going to threaten to fire me if—'

'I told you before I'd never do that, Olivia.' His voice was hard, but then his expression lightened as he offered her a wry smile. 'I'm not the kind of man who resorts to coercion or bribery. I have better strategies than that.'

'Which are?'

'I simply intend to convince you of the benefits of marriage to me.'

'The benefits,' she repeated. Already she could imagine all too well just what some of those benefits might be: waking up next to Aziz every morning; sleeping in his arms every night; sating that wild need she'd felt for him in the garden again and again…

'I think,' he murmured, his smile turning sleepy, 'Judging by your blush, you might be aware of some of them?'

'Damn you,' she choked, and turned away again, if only to hide her flushed cheeks.

'Olivia.' She felt his hand on her shoulder, the heat of his body behind hers. 'I'm not trying to embarrass you. Trust me, the attraction we feel for one another, as unexpected as it might be for both of us, is something I certainly consider a benefit.'

'You don't marry someone just because you're attracted to them,' Olivia managed to get out. Her voice sounded suffocated.

'No, of course not. But it's better to be attracted to the person you marry, don't you think?'

'Were you—are you—attracted to Elena?' Olivia asked and Aziz didn't answer. She turned around, rubbing her arms as if she was cold. And she was cold, despite the still, drowsy air in the room. She was cold with shock—not just over Aziz's proposal but her own reaction to it. For when he'd told her he wanted to marry her, as disbelieving as she'd been, a part of her had already answered with a resounding *yes*. A part of her had clamoured that this, *he*, was what she'd been waiting for, what she needed.

'I didn't spend enough time with Elena to discover whether we were attracted to one another,' Aziz finally said. 'The two times we met were akin to business meetings. Neither of us was interested in anything else.'

'But weren't you curious if you'd even like each other, never mind desire—?'

Aziz sighed. 'Why are we talking about Elena?'

'Because you were planning to marry her,' Olivia shot back. 'And, if by some miracle she walked through the door right now, you'd still marry her.' She shook her head, scrambling for self-preservation. 'Although, you're right, I'm not sure why we're talking about Elena, or any of this. I'm not going to marry you, Aziz. I can't.'

He raised his eyebrows, a small smile playing about his mouth. 'Can't or won't?'

'Both.'

Aziz gazed at her thoughtfully, his face calm, his whole being utterly unruffled. 'Are you happy in Paris, Olivia?'

'What?' Her nails dug into her arms as she hugged herself then, realising what she was doing, she dropped her arms and glared at him. 'What kind of question is that?' A good one, she thought with something close to panic. And one whose answer she refused to give.

'Because you admitted to me in the garden today that you chose the life you live because it's safe. Because anything else is too hard.'

'So?' she demanded, her voice raw, and Aziz smiled gently.

'So I'm offering you an alternative. One that is still safe but might be more pleasant, more enjoyable, than the life you currently lead. Aren't you ever lonely?'

'You don't marry someone just because you're lonely.'

'I'm sure lots of people marry for precisely that reason.'

'Well, I don't.' He didn't respond, just sat there, watching her. Waiting. 'Your suggestion is absurd,' she burst out. 'As if I would marry you simply because I'm a little lonely sometimes!' She shook her head, furious now. 'You're unbelievably arrogant.'

'Arrogant? But I don't mind admitting it, Olivia. I'm lonely too.'

'The Gentleman Playboy?' she scoffed. 'Lonely?'

'None of the liaisons I've had have been remotely satisfying except in the most basic way.'

'And you want more than that?'

'Not exactly, which is why I think we'll suit each other so well.'

'I don't understand.'

'Don't you?' Aziz gave her a fleeting, almost sad smile. Olivia shook her head, not wanting to understand. Not wanting to concede any point to Aziz.

'We're friends, I hope,' he resumed. 'And we're attracted to each other—both a solid basis for a marriage.'

'Maybe,' she allowed, but even that felt like conceding too much. Was he going to argue her into agreeing? Knowing how persuasive he could be, and how tempted she was, he just might.

Rather frantically she reminded herself of all the reasons she shouldn't entertain this idea: she barely knew him, for one. He was a playboy, for a second. And third, he was ruler of a country. She'd have to be a queen, a public figure, and just that thought nearly had her breaking out in hives.

There was no way she wanted to bind herself to a life like that, never mind the man involved.

Of course she wasn't thinking of it. Not for one second.

She shook her head again and Aziz smiled. 'In a moment,' he said teasingly, 'I think I'm going to see smoke coming out of your ears.'

'I just find it so incredible that you would ever suggest such a thing,' Olivia forced out.

Aziz tilted his head to one side, his gaze sweeping over her. 'Do you really find it incredible, Olivia?'

'You mean because you're desperate,' she answered flatly. 'I'm the only choice you have.'

'That's not quite true. I'm sure I could find someone else at short notice if I really needed to.'

'Am I meant to be flattered that you chose me?'

'Flattered, no. But I would like you to seriously consider the idea instead of rejecting it out of hand, outraged that I even suggested such a thing.'

She felt some of her anger leave her, and she missed the certainty it had given her. When you were so busy being angry you didn't have time to think, to wonder.

To want.

She took a breath, let it out slowly and then sat on the sofa across from Aziz. 'All right, fine. Tell me what you're thinking, Aziz. Tell me just how you envision a marriage between us working.' If she couldn't dissuade him through outrage, Olivia thought, she'd do it through cold, hard logic. She'd argue him into rescinding his offer.

Liar. The only person who was likely to change her mind was her. She was playing with fire, having this conversation. Entertaining the idea of marriage to Aziz even for a moment made it far more likely that she'd end up with burned fingers—and a broken heart.

Because, while Aziz was waking her up to ideas of life, love and happiness, she was under no illusion about what he still wanted: a convenient marriage. A cold one.

'I confess, I haven't thought through every detail,' Aziz told her, his voice low and steady. 'But that's something we can do together.'

'Don't jump ahead,' Olivia answered sharply. 'I just want to hear what you're thinking, Aziz. For curiosity's sake.'

'For curiosity's sake,' he repeated, his eyes and smile both gleaming. 'Very well. I imagine it would look something like this. Tomorrow we both show up in the Gold Salon here in the palace. We say some vows. We become husband and wife.' He spread his hands. 'The rest is up for discussion.'

Not everything, Olivia thought. Although, why she even

cared she didn't know. She'd been thinking about taking a *class*, for heaven's sake. Not getting married.

'Don't make light of it,' she told him. 'It's a serious thing. I'd take any vows I said seriously.'

'So would I, Olivia. But are you seriously thinking about saying them? Or are you really just curious?'

She stared at him, unwilling to answer. *Why* was she pursuing this conversation? *Actually thinking...* 'It's mad,' she said finally and he nodded.

'I know.'

'I don't want to be a queen, a public figure.'

'Your appearances could be kept to a minimum. Your privacy and comfort would be paramount.'

She shook her head. 'The last thing I want is to live in a strange country, far from everything I've known.'

'Something we can discuss. If you married me, you could divide your time between Paris and Kadar.'

'But you would be in Kadar.'

'Yes.'

So he really was suggesting the kind of arrangement he'd had with Elena: convenient, cold, coming together only for special engagements or state functions.

And yet in the space of about five minutes, against all sense, not to mention her better judgement, she had been spinning some other fantasy. Picturing herself waking up in Aziz's bed, halfway to falling in love...

'I'm not sure,' she said as crisply as she could, 'What I am meant to gain from such an arrangement.'

'Companionship, for one. Physical affection.' His smile was gently teasing but Olivia just stared him down.

'Companionship, Aziz, with half the world between us? Besides, what kind of companionship can two strangers really hope to have? I said it last night and I'll say it again—you don't really know me.'

He tilted his head, his smile almost sad, somehow. 'Don't I?'

He knew her better than anyone else did, but that still wasn't saying all that much. 'No,' she said, her voice still crisp. 'You don't.'

'I know you prefer coffee in the mornings but tea in the afternoons. You can't stand the smell of fish. You dress in dark colours but you like bright ones. You jiggle your left foot when you're nervous.' Both of their gazes moved to her jiggling foot and with an exasperated breath she placed both feet flat on the floor.

'I commend your powers of observation, but none of that is really knowing me.' Although she was more shaken than she would ever admit at how much he'd observed about her. How did he know all those things? She didn't think she could say she knew the same about him, and she had a feeling Aziz liked it that way.

'Fine.' His expression was bland and yet somehow challenging. Or perhaps she was just feeling remarkably raw. 'You like a quiet life.'

'I *told* you that.'

'But you didn't always. You loved someone once, and you don't ever want to love again. You have secrets but you want to pretend you don't. You have a deliciously dirty laugh but no one ever hears it.'

'Stop,' she whispered.

'You bought a red and purple scarf but you won't wear it out of the house. You hum pop songs from ten years ago when you're working, but you couldn't tell me a single hit song from today. You don't play the piano very often, but when you do your soul and all its sorrows pours right out of you.' He sat back on the sofa, his arms folded, one eyebrow arched. 'Well? How am I doing so far?'

'If you think,' Olivia said in a shaky whisper, 'That

knowing all that about me will convince me to marry you, you're dead wrong, Aziz.'

'Because you don't want to be known.' He nodded, as if he'd expected as much, his gaze blazing and so very certain. 'So you can't use that as an argument, can you, Olivia? That I don't know you. Because you don't even want me to.'

Except she didn't know *what* she wanted any more. She looked away from him, unable to bear the certainty she saw in his eyes. 'So why,' she demanded, 'Would I want to marry you?'

'I told you. Companionship. Attraction.' He paused. 'Sex.' That one word seemed to sizzle in the air like hot grease on a griddle. 'Closeness,' Aziz continued, 'But not too close.' He leaned forward and reluctantly Olivia looked back at him. 'That's what we both want, isn't it? Enough, but not too much?'

'I'm not even sure what that means.'

'Then let me enlighten you. It means I'll let you keep your secrets, and I'll keep mine. It means I'll make love to you every night, but I won't ask you questions or press you for answers. I won't fall in love with you and I won't break your heart.'

Olivia pressed one hand against her thundering heart. The words, she knew, were meant to comfort her, but they just sounded cold. Maybe it was more than the half-life she'd had, but would it be enough? Did she even dare to want—and try for—more? 'And you assume I want that kind of—arrangement,' she stated numbly.

Aziz arched an eyebrow. 'By your own admission, you're not looking for love. And neither am I.'

Disappointment was like a stone in her stomach. 'Why aren't you?'

He shrugged. 'Same reason as you, I suppose, except I never got as far as actually loving someone.'

'If you haven't had your heart broken, why are you so afraid of getting hurt?'

'A child's heart, perhaps,' he answered after a moment. 'Not the same thing.'

'You mean your father.'

'My experience with him made me reluctant to love or trust anyone else.'

'Was he—was he cruel to you?'

'It doesn't matter,' he dismissed. 'We're talking about the future, Olivia. What we can gain from each other.'

She folded her arms. 'And what if…?' *What if I told you I wanted more?* No, she couldn't ask that. Couldn't reveal that much. 'What if I told you I like my life the way it is?'

'You could tell me, but I'm not sure I'd believe it.'

She opened her mouth to tell him off for his arrogance, but nothing came out. She was suddenly and utterly tired of the posturing. The pretence. *The lies.*

'Fine. Maybe I'm missing something, but I'm not sure what you're offering will fill that emptiness.'

'You could try.'

'And if it doesn't work?'

'Then you can go back to Paris and live the life you had before. You'll be married to me, I admit, but I won't trouble you.'

Which just made her feel sadder than ever. Sudden tears stung her eyes and she turned away, hiding her face from him, trying to hide all of herself, but she knew it was too late. He'd seen too much.

'You've been hurt before, Olivia,' Aziz said quietly. 'I understand that and I respect it. I promise you, I won't hurt you.'

'You can't make promises like that.'

'To the very best of my ability.'

'It's not enough.' She dragged a breath into her lungs. 'You've got the wrong end of the stick anyway,' she forced out. 'I haven't had my heart broken in the way you think, by some *man*.'

Aziz stilled, his expression turning watchful, alert. 'Who was it, then?'

Olivia blinked back more tears, her gaze unfocused, her mind spinning. She remembered the last time she'd talked about Daniel, when her father had told her to forget him. *For ever.* Yet now, incredibly, she wanted to talk about him. She wanted to tell Aziz, to have him understand...

Madness.

'Olivia,' he said, and just the way he said her name made her feel he understood, or at least that he could understand if she let him. And she wanted to let him; she craved another person's compassion.

'His name was Daniel,' she said clearly. She lifted her head to meet Aziz's concerned gaze. 'And he was my son.'

CHAPTER NINE

IT WASN'T WHAT he'd been expecting. A son. A *child*. Aziz stared at Olivia, at the grief he saw so clearly in her eyes, on her face, and thought, *of course*. Of course she hadn't had some standard, run-of-the-mill love affair. Of course her pain was deeper than that.

He leaned forward and put his hand over hers; her skin was icy cold. 'I'm sorry,' he said quietly, and she let out a sound that was close to a sob. Everything in Aziz ached. 'Tell me?' he said, a question, and she stared down at their hands, his skin brown and hers so pale. He thought she wouldn't say anything but after a moment she began to speak.

'I was seventeen.' She took a deep breath and looked up at him, her eyes glassy with tears, her face pale. 'I've never told anyone this,' she said in a low voice. 'Not one person.'

'You can tell me, Olivia,' he told her quietly. 'If you want to. If you think it might help.'

'I don't know.' She withdrew her hand from his and wrapped her arms around herself, as if she was cold. Aziz felt the sudden, fierce need to put his arms around her, to warm her and comfort her in a way that had nothing to do with desire but rather with compassion—or even some deeper emotion. 'I don't even like to think of Daniel,' she whispered. 'It hurts too much.'

'What happened to him?'

He thought she wouldn't answer. Her gaze had become distant and unfocused, her slender arms still wrapped around her body as if she were holding herself in; keeping herself together. 'I gave him away,' she whispered, and her voice broke on the last word. She bowed her head, her shoulders shaking, and Aziz didn't even think then. He just acted.

He pulled her into his arms, felt her slender body shaking with sobs. She didn't pull away; if anything, she pressed closer against him, needing him in a way that flooded Aziz with a longing to comfort and protect her.

When had someone needed him, wanted him, for anything other than a casual sexual encounter? He'd chosen things that way, had told himself he preferred it, but as he held Olivia close he began to grasp just how much he'd been missing.

And still would miss. The kind of marriage he'd suggested to Olivia wasn't meant to be about this kind of intimacy: sharing secrets, offering each other comfort. Already they were both breaking the rules and Aziz knew that couldn't lead to anywhere good.

'It was an accident, of course,' Olivia said after a moment, her voice muffled against his chest. He could feel the dampness of her tears through his shirt. 'I didn't even have a boyfriend at the time. I went to a party and had too much to drink. I didn't normally drink at all, besides wine sometimes at a family dinner. But I was feeling grown up—I'd just been offered a place at university—and there was a boy there I'd always had a secret crush on. Maybe not so secret, though.' She let out a laugh that held no humour and shook her head.

Aziz felt all his protective instincts rear up. 'You're

saying this boy took advantage of you while you were drunk? That's rape, Olivia.'

'No, I wasn't that drunk,' she told him. 'Honestly. I'd just had enough to feel prettier and funnier and more confident than I actually was. And when one thing led to another…' She sighed, the sound heavy, even defeated. 'I regretted it, of course, in the morning. Terribly. I never even thought about falling pregnant, though. Stupidly.'

'And when you found out?' Aziz asked in a low voice.

'I didn't find out. My mother did. She suspected before I did, at least. I was sick in the mornings, and I thought I just had stomach flu. She confronted me and my first thought was that I just *couldn't* be. But, of course, I was.'

'And what happened then?'

'My mother was furious. We lived in South America then, and the country was conservative, the ex-pat community very small. She insisted I get a termination. She told me it was for the best, as I already had a university place, my whole life in front of me. And I convinced myself she was right.'

'But you didn't get a termination,' Aziz stated quietly. 'Did you? Because you said you gave him away.'

Olivia let out a shuddering breath and nodded, her hair brushing against his chest. 'No, I didn't, but I almost did. My mother had arranged it all. We had to go to New York, because terminations were illegal where we living. She made up this big story about a mother-daughter shopping trip. She didn't want my father to know.'

'Why not?'

'She said it would kill him.' Her voice choked. 'Not literally, of course. But I was always a daddy's girl. Spoiled, probably, but I—I loved my father so much. I couldn't bear the thought of disappointing him, so I agreed not to tell him.' She was quiet for a moment, so he could hear the soft draw and tear of her breaths. 'He used to have me play piano whenever he was tired. He said my music always soothed him. My mother said he wouldn't be able to bear hearing about what I'd done. And she wouldn't let me tell Jeremy—the father—either. Not that he would have even cared, but…he should have known. I should have been strong enough to tell him.'

Aziz couldn't bear to hear the throb of grief in Olivia's voice. He sensed her sorrow had more than one cause: the loss of her son, the secret from her father, her mother's fury, the stupid boy's rejection of her; all of it had tangled together, choking her, keeping her from truly living.

'So we went to New York,' Olivia resumed after a moment, her voice flat now. 'And I made it all the way to the clinic. All the way to the examining room, even. The whole time I felt as if it were all happening to someone else, almost as if I were watching a film, wondering what was going to happen next. And then the doctor came in—she was very kind—and asked me if I understood what was happening. I've never known if she asked that of everyone, or if I just looked particularly terrified.'

'I imagine,' Aziz murmured against her hair, 'It was a terrifying experience.'

'I told the doctor that I understood, but I couldn't go through with it. My mother was out in the waiting room and when I came out after just a few minutes she was furious. *Furious.*'

'Your mother sounds like a fearsome woman.'

'I can't blame her, really. She was doing her best for me—trying to protect me, I suppose, along with our family's reputation. My father's career.' Her voice choked again and she took a few even breaths before she continued. 'My father has always been such a dreamer. He needs someone like her, I think, although…' She stopped, and Aziz wondered what she was thinking. Remembering.

'What happened then?' he asked after a moment.

'I told her I wanted to keep the baby. She told me I was wrecking my life. We were at a stand-off for a while, the rest of my first trimester anyway. I remember because I felt him kick for the first time and I still didn't know what was going to happen to him or me.'

Aziz's chest hurt as he imagined her with one hand pressed to her gently rounded belly, overwhelmed with both wonder and despair. 'Oh, Olivia.'

'My mother wanted me to give him up for adoption. She still insisted on hiding my pregnancy from everyone—she planned to tell people I was recovering from stress and send me to a clinic in America to have the baby.'

It sounded like a selfish, heartless decision and inwardly he railed against the woman who had bullied her daughter in such a way. 'Is that what you did?'

A small hesitation, a telling pause. 'Yes,' she finally said. 'I gave in eventually, so I went.'

He wondered what she'd chosen not to tell him, but decided not to ask. 'How long were you there?'

'Six months. The longest six months of my life in some ways, and the shortest in others. Because I knew I'd have to give him up when it was over. I wasn't…I wasn't strong enough to have him on my own. I should have been, but I wasn't.'

'You were so young, Olivia.'

'Yes, but other girls have done it. I could have—I don't know—applied for benefits or childcare help at university. I could have stood up to my mother and insisted. But I didn't do any of that. I just felt so numb, so dead inside. I didn't have the strength.'

His arms tightened around her. 'Tell me what happened next.'

'He was born. He was so beautiful…' She swallowed hard. 'I held him after he was born. He was so tiny, he fitted right in the crook of my arm. He looked like a little old man.' She let out a sound that was half-laugh, half-sob. 'I kept him overnight. I even fed him myself, though the nurses told me it would better if I didn't. I remember staring down at his face. He kept looking at me with these huge blue eyes when I fed him. He was so alert.' She drew a shuddering breath. 'I named him, even though I knew it would be changed. Daniel.'

She pressed her face into Aziz's chest once more. 'And then I let him go.' She drew a quick, sharp breath, her words coming faster, tumbling over themselves. 'I believe he's happy now. I pray he is. An American couple adopted him. I met them, and they seemed very nice. Very kind. He'll be well looked after.'

'But you didn't want to give him up.'

'No.' She subsided then, still leaning against him, and Aziz wondered if she was even aware that he was holding her—that he *wanted* to hold her. 'I never did, but I tried to convince myself it was for the best. I told myself I had university to look forward to, a career as a musician. My mother kept telling me to forget about it, him, because I still had my whole life in front of me. It just didn't feel that way. It felt like my life had gone. And it was my own fault.'

'It wasn't, Olivia. You were young—'

'So? Does that really make a difference? If you want something badly enough, you should be strong enough to fight for it.'

He didn't argue with her any more, because he understood how she felt. He knew how you could tell yourself the truth so many times—*it's not my fault my father doesn't like me; I'm worthy and deserving of love in my own right*—and yet you still didn't believe it. Maybe you never could.

And Olivia, he surmised, had been devastated by this experience. *Losing her son.* No wonder she hid herself away, longed only for a quiet life. She'd been hurt badly and she didn't want to try again. Could he blame her? He was the same, and he hadn't even been as hurt as she had. He hadn't lost as much.

'So what happened after?' he asked. 'You went to university...'

'For one term. I don't remember much about it, actually. I was kind of—numb.' She eased herself away from him then, and he missed her warmth and softness pressing against him. She scooted across the sofa, her arms folded across her chest, her head bent and her hair hanging down so he couldn't see the expression on her face.

'I dropped out after Christmas,' she continued. 'And I drifted around for a while. Then my father arranged the housekeeping position. He was trying to help me.'

Again Aziz sensed there was something she wasn't saying but he had no idea what it was. 'And you haven't wanted anything else?' he said after a moment.

'No.' She rose from the sofa and paced restlessly to the window, one slender hand resting on the sill, her back to him. 'I don't know why I told you all this. The point of anything between us was that we'd get to keep our secrets, wasn't it?'

He sat back against the sofa and watched her; her narrow back seemed almost to quiver with tension. 'Maybe not the *point*. More like a side benefit.'

'And yet I just told you mine.'

'Are you sorry you did?'

She turned to him, one hand still on the sill, her eyes dark and wide. 'No, I'm not. Which is kind of frightening.'

Yes, Aziz agreed silently, it was. For both of them. Hearing someone's secrets meant they trusted you to keep them. Not to let them down. And, while he'd promised he wouldn't hurt her, suddenly it seemed harder now and far more fearsome. He really didn't want to hurt her, not even a tiny bit. He cared about her, more than he'd expected. More than he wanted to.

'And this kind of soul-baring certainly isn't part of any arrangement we might have, is it?' she asked with a humourless smile. 'Have I freaked you out?'

'No, of course not. And, in any case, I said everything was up for discussion,' Aziz answered as lightly as he could.

She raised her eyebrows. 'You still want to marry me?'

'Yes.' And he knew he meant it, even if nothing had happened quite as he'd expected. Even if he wasn't sure what a marriage between them would look like now or what he really wanted from it.

She shook her head and turned back to the window. 'It's just so crazy,' she murmured. 'So, so crazy.'

'I completely agree. But my father's will is crazy.'

'Would you ever have married,' she asked, 'If the will hadn't dictated it?'

He hesitated, not sure what she wanted to hear, and uncertain how much truth to share. 'I don't know,' he finally said, which was, at least, honest.

'What about an heir? You'll need one eventually, I suppose?'

'Yes.'

She tensed then, her fingers curling around the windowsill, knuckles whitening. 'So this marriage—it would mean children?'

And that, Aziz realised, was a bit of a loaded issue. 'Yes, Olivia, it would.' Something he hadn't mentioned before—hadn't even thought of, really, except in the abstract. He waited for her to say something, but she just stared out of the window. 'How do you feel about that?' he asked after a moment.

'A baby,' she murmured, then shook her head again. 'I—I don't know.'

'Do you want more children?'

'I never thought...' She lapsed into silence and Aziz just waited. Just like Olivia, he was starting to realise just all a marriage between them would entail. He'd thought he'd understood and accepted it all after having discussed it with Elena; they'd laid out all the relevant points in a twenty-page legal document. He'd accepted that a cold business arrangement was what he wanted for himself, never mind what he needed to fulfil the terms of his father's will.

But now...with Olivia... When he'd wiped away her tears, when he'd held her in his arms, when he'd felt her pain...

He couldn't let himself want more. Olivia didn't want to love him, and he didn't want to love her. They needed to keep it that way. Keep it simple. Keep it safe.

'I can't give you an answer now,' she said finally. 'It's too big a decision. I know you have to marry by tomorrow, and I can tell you later today, perhaps. But I can't...' She shook her head, biting her lip.

'I understand,' Aziz said quietly. It was a huge decision, for both of them. And, just as Olivia had pointed out earlier, it was a case of needs must for him, but not for her.

She turned to him. 'What will you do if I say no?'

'That's not your problem to worry about, Olivia. And frankly I'd rather you didn't agree just because you're trying to save me.' He smiled wryly, although he felt a certain heaviness inside. He couldn't stand the thought of her pity. 'This isn't a mercy mission.'

'I know that.'

'Any marriage between us would, I hope, benefit you as much as it would me.' Although he wasn't sure if he believed that. What did he really have to offer Olivia? Sex? She could get it somewhere else if she wanted it. Friendship? If she wanted friends, she could make them. She didn't need to get *married*, for heaven's sake.

So what would motivate her to agree? What was making her think seriously about it now?

And then he knew. Of course—a child. She wanted a child.

Not him; not his friendship or even just his body. Only a child. A child of her own.

'Think about it,' he said, and his voice sounded strange, stilted. He forced a smile. 'You know where to find me when you have your answer.'

She nodded slowly, and after an endless moment she turned and left the room.

Aziz remained seated, staring, his mind spinning emptily. Distantly he wondered how he would feel if Olivia now agreed to marry him. And with a heaviness inside he knew it wouldn't be the unadulterated relief he'd been anticipating just a few moments ago—and he didn't even want to figure out why.

Olivia walked slowly down the corridor, barely aware of where she was going. Somehow she found her way back to her bedroom, which thankfully was empty. She didn't think she could face seeing anyone just now, not even Mada or Abra with their kind, smiling faces.

She sank onto the bed, her mind still spinning, emotional and physical exhaustion crashing over her in a tidal wave.

What had just happened?

The events of the last few hours swirled through her mind, from her passionate kiss with Aziz in the royal gardens, to his shocking marriage proposal, to her own just as shocking admission. *She'd told him about Daniel.* She'd cried in front of him, had sought his comfort, had revelled in the feel of his arms around her. *She was seriously thinking about accepting his marriage proposal.*

She'd said it was madness, and he'd agreed. It *was* madness. She barely knew him. She'd have to be a *queen*, appearing in public, photographed by newspapers when all she'd ever wanted was a quiet, solitary life.

She'd have a child.

Another child—not one to replace Daniel, because no baby could ever do that, but one to keep and love, one to redeem both her past and herself. One to cherish...

Olivia told herself she could have a child without getting married. Women did it all the time; you didn't even need a man any more, just a sperm bank. She was half-amazed she hadn't thought of it before, yet the prospect held no appeal now. She wanted a child, yes, but she knew she wanted more than that. She wanted an equal, loving partner to support her and help raise their child.

And how on earth could that be Aziz? He'd just laid out all the reasons he didn't want a real, loving marriage. She was heading for heartbreak at a hundred miles an hour and the only way to stop was to get on a plane to Paris.

But the thought of going back to Paris now felt like regression. Defeat. She couldn't go back, not to the life she'd once had, and not to the little better than that life she'd been thinking of.

She wanted more. She wanted it all. But it was madness to try for it with Aziz.

Wasn't it?

Aziz had made it clear he wasn't looking to love or be loved. *Enough and no more*, he'd said. But how much was enough?

A tremor ran through her body as she once again remembered that incredible kiss…and imagined being with Aziz as a wife, a lover. The feel of his hands on her body, his mouth on hers…

With a shuddery breath Olivia lay down on the bed and stared at the canopy above her. Could she really be thinking about marrying Aziz?

She rolled onto her side, tucked her legs up to her chest and closed her eyes. *Madness*, she told herself. *Madness*. He'd already stirred up so many feelings and desires inside her. How much more of a maelstrom would he create in her if she married him?

Even if they set limits on their relationship, kept to simply being friends, it wouldn't work.

Would it?

Or could she keep herself from feeling too much, from falling in love with him? She'd kept herself from feeling anything at all for ten years. Surely she could manage it?

Did she really have any choice?

With a jolt Olivia realised she'd already decided. Of course she had. She wasn't going to go back to a half-life of safety, numbness and fear. Aziz had changed her too much already for that. And, if she wasn't going to go back, she had to go forward. She wanted what Aziz offered: friendship, physical affection, *a child*.

It was so much more than she'd ever had in her adult

life and it would have to be enough. She would make it be enough, Olivia told herself. She would choose joy.

A sudden bubble of incredulous wonder rose up inside her, escaped in a gurgle of sound—although whether it was a laugh, a sob or something in between Olivia didn't know.

Because, while she was choosing life, hope and happiness, she had no idea what that would actually look like. Feel like. And even more alarmingly, she was quite sure that Aziz wasn't choosing the same things.

Aziz paced the confines of his study, as he'd been doing for the last hour since Olivia had left him. He was going to wear the carpet to threads, he thought wryly, then let out an impatient sigh as he glanced at the clock.

How much time should he give her? And what the hell was he going to do if she said no?

He walked to the window, bracing his hands on the sill as the evening breeze, only just beginning to cool, blew over him. The trouble was, he didn't just want some nameless bride to fulfil the terms of his father's will any more. If Olivia refused his proposal, he could most likely find someone else to marry him. He'd sign another legal document that covered every eventuality; he'd work hard to make sure his bride was accepted by his people.

But he didn't want to do that any more; he was amazed that he'd ever wanted it, that he'd been willing to enter an utterly soulless agreement with Elena.

And what are you going to have with Olivia, if she agrees?

Aziz pushed away from the window and paced restlessly once more. The afternoon with Olivia had blown all his preconceptions, all his priorities, to hell. Their passionate kiss. Her heartbroken confession. The feel of her in his arms, her hair brushing against his cheek, her tears wetting his shirt.

Just the memory made him ache in a way he hadn't ached since he was a boy desperate to gain his father's approval. *His love.*

Was he going to be so phenomenally stupid as to go down that path again? Try to make someone love him, someone who didn't, and didn't even want to? Who had *said* as much?

No, of course not. He'd learned his lesson, surely. And, while he might feel tender and protective towards Olivia when she was obviously in a vulnerable state, he wasn't about to love her. Of course he wasn't.

If he married her, he'd give her what he'd promised. Companionship. Children. Loyalty.

But not love. Never love.

A sound at the doorway startled him and he turned, his heart seeming to leap into his throat and then still completely as he saw Olivia standing there. She still wore the plain trousers and tailored shirt she'd had on earlier, but they looked slightly crumpled now, and her hair was loose and dark about her face. The dye, Aziz noticed, was already starting to fade; he could see streaks of caramel through the black, the real Olivia coming through.

'Good evening.' He cleared his throat and forced a light smile as he raised his eyebrows in teasing query. 'You look rather serious, Olivia.'

'I feel rather serious,' she answered quietly. She stepped into the room, closing the door behind her. 'Malik said I could find you here. I hope I'm not disturbing you?'

'No, of course not.' He'd just been waiting for her to find him for the last hour. 'Have you made a decision?'

'Yes.'

He smiled, shoved his hands into his trouser pockets and rocked on his heels. 'Well, don't keep me in suspense.'

'I don't mean to. It's just—it's a bit like leaping off a cliff, isn't it, Aziz? And you have no idea what waits for you at the bottom.'

His heart lurched, although whether in relief or hope or even fear he didn't know. Wouldn't consider. 'Is that a yes, Olivia?'

'Yes.' Her lips trembled even as she smiled. 'It is a yes. But I have a lot of questions, Aziz. A lot of concerns.'

'Of course you do. And, like I said, everything is up for discussion. We can make this work for both of us, I promise.'

'I told you before, you can't make promises like that.'

'I can.' He stepped towards her; the emotion rushing through him, he realised, was more than relief or hope. It was something frighteningly close to joy. 'I can and I will. We'll discuss anything you like. But not just this minute.'

She blinked up at him; he'd stepped closer so he was standing right in front of her. 'Why not?'

'Because right now I just want to kiss you. My bride.'

Her lips parted in both surprise and expectation and Aziz placed his hands on her shoulders, drawing her gently towards him. Her hair whispered against his face and her breath came out on a sigh as he dipped his head and brushed his lips against hers.

Oh, he'd wanted this again. He'd been waiting for it, dreaming of it, since he'd last kissed her. Both kisses reached a place inside him he'd thought had been closed off for ever. His heart. His soul. Everything in him wanted her, needed her, with an urgency that shocked him even as it made him bolder, deepening the kiss, pulling him against her so she could feel his arousal.

'Aziz…' His name was a moan as his tongue swept the softness of her mouth, his hand sliding down to cup the gentle swell of her breast.

He felt her sudden indrawn breath against his mouth and he broke the kiss, his heart thudding as he managed a wry smile. 'I don't think we'll have any problems in that department,' he murmured. 'You drive me wild, Olivia.'

'It's mutual.' She flushed as she straightened her clothes then gazed up at him, searching his face with a worried, wide-eyed gaze. 'Can we really do this?'

Aziz cocked an eyebrow. 'To what, exactly, are you referring?'

Olivia let out a hiccupy laugh and shook her head. 'You know what I meant. This *marriage*.'

'Of course we can.'

He drew her back into his arms, needing her to be there. Right now he didn't want to discuss the practicalities, or make promises about how they wouldn't hurt each other. Wouldn't love each other.

Right now, he just wanted to kiss her again, so he did.

CHAPTER TEN

OLIVIA SAT AT the head of a large mahogany table, Aziz next to her, a pack of lawyers at the other end, a host of legal documents spread out on the table before them.

Her wedding was in one hour.

After Aziz's kisses last night, he was all business this morning, dressed in a grey silk suit, a pair of glasses perched on his nose as he scanned a legal document whose endless tiny type had blurred in front of Olivia's eyes.

Looking at him now, he seemed forbiddingly remote. A stranger. She hadn't even known he wore glasses. Such a small thing, so unimportant, and yet in that moment it seemed critical. It reminded her rather painfully how little she knew this man, and yet after spending just forty-eight hours with him she was willing to pledge her life to him. Be mother to his child.

Which was what she needed to remember now, she told herself. Forget fairy tales, the castles in the air she'd been building in her head for the last twenty-four hours. She needed to remember what she was getting out of this bargain: companionship. Affection. *A child.* She would have a child.

Aziz, she thought suddenly, would make a good father. He would laugh and tease and tickle.

Do you really know what kind of father he'll be? What

kind of husband he'll be? What on earth are you doing, Olivia?

'Looking at point five...' one of the lawyers said, clearing his throat, and Olivia snapped back to attention.

'Yes,' she murmured, gazing blindly down at her copy of the agreement, although she had no idea what point five, or any of the points, was.

Aziz leaned over and flipped the page over, tapping one lean finger in the relevant place.

'Thank you,' Olivia murmured, flushing. Point five, it turned out, dealt with her royal appearances, 'as and when required'.

'We can put a limit on them,' Aziz said, turning to her. 'No more than once a month, if you prefer.' He spoke calmly, unemotionally, as if this was no more than a normal business meeting. It made Olivia feel like screaming.

She should be reassured by all the provisions Aziz was putting in place, she told herself. He was looking out for her, protecting her interests. She should want all these safeguards, because then she would know just what she was getting into.

Except she didn't know what she was getting into, didn't even know what she *wanted* to get into. Last night she'd told herself she'd chosen joy. She'd acknowledged how alive and whole and happy Aziz made her feel, and had made herself believe a marriage with him could work because it was still more than she'd ever had before. Had ever dared to have.

This morning she didn't know anything.

'Olivia?' Aziz prompted.

'Once a month is fine.'

'Very well.' He turned towards the team of lawyers. 'Could you add that, please?'

'As for point six...' one of the lawyers said, and Olivia

forced herself to focus on the next point, even though her mind was buzzing and the words blurred. She made out 'issue resulting' and she turned to Aziz.

'Issue?'

'Children,' he murmured and her fingers tightened on the papers.

'What is the provision for our children?'

'We can discuss it, of course. This document is based on the one that was drawn up for Elena and me, but naturally things are different now.'

Not that different, Olivia thought with a clawing panic. This was still a convenient marriage. A cold-hearted business arrangement.

Was she selling her soul for a little happiness? Settling for a little more than a half-life, but still not enough?

The questions screamed inside her head so loudly she felt like covering her ears. That wouldn't help. Nothing would help.

She forced herself to look at Aziz. His expression was impossible to read. 'What was your agreement with Elena, with regards to children?' she asked. Her voice sounded distant and strange.

'We both needed heirs, so that was our priority. The first son would be the heir to Kadar, the child after the heir to Thallia.'

'What if you didn't have a son?'

He gave a small shrug. 'Just about every king has faced that possibility. Perhaps by the time a child of mine accedes the throne, a woman could rule Kadar. I certainly hope so.'

She took a deep breath. 'Any child of ours would remain in our home and not be sent away to school.'

Aziz nodded calmly. 'Make a note, please,' he told the lawyers.

'No nannies or governesses.'

'We would need some childcare provision, Olivia. You will have some royal responsibilities, even if they are kept to a minimum.'

'Fine. Any childcare provider must be approved by me.'

'And me,' he answered lightly. 'Fair?'

She nodded jerkily, hating that everything had to be a negotiation. Hating how cold it all felt, when all she wanted to do was throw herself into Aziz's arms and beg him to love her.

Love her? Was that what she really wanted now? Was that why she was so panicked?

He gazed at her thoughtfully for a moment, his eyes narrowed, and then he nodded towards the lawyers. 'Could you leave us for a moment?'

With murmured apologies and assents they left, the door clicking shut behind them. Aziz rose from the table.

'What's wrong, Olivia?'

She clenched her hands, her nails biting into the skin of her palms. 'Nothing's wrong.'

'Are you having second thoughts?' He stood there quietly, his arms folded. He didn't look angry or uncaring, just…calm. Too calm. As if he was in a business meeting, which Olivia knew he *was*.

'Not second thoughts,' she said after a moment. 'Not exactly. But this is so *strange*, Aziz. And now that we're talking about all these details it makes it seem even stranger. More real and less real at the same time.'

'So you *are* having second thoughts.'

'I—I don't know!' She whirled away from him, suddenly near tears. Her emotions were so close to the surface now. They'd been buried deep for a decade, yet now the feelings bubbled up, impossible to suppress.

'Olivia.' Aziz came to stand behind her, his hands resting gently on her shoulders. 'I know this is strange. It's strange for me, too. But that doesn't mean it can't work—'

'Like a washing machine?' she filled in. 'Like a...a *blender*?' She let out a laugh that sounded half-wild and jerked out of his arms. He stared at her, frowning slightly.

'That's not the analogy I would have chosen, but I suppose it is appropriate.' She shook her head, the movement as wild as her laugh, and his gaze narrowed. 'What's really going on here, Olivia? Analogies aside, what's bothering you? What are you afraid of?'

'I'm not afraid.' Except, she was. She was afraid of all these feelings inside her, feelings Aziz had called up. Afraid of caring too much, of getting hurt.

Afraid of falling in love with him.

Last night, when he'd been kissing her and making his promises, caring about Aziz hadn't seemed so scary a possibility. Today, when he stood in front of her in a business suit and with a narrowed gaze, it was terrifying.

'There's just so much uncertainty,' she said after a long, tense moment when Aziz just gazed at her with that inscrutable expression. 'What if the people of Kadar don't accept me? They think I'm Elena right now. What if they really want Elena? What if they decide they want Khalil because you lied to them about this?'

Aziz's jaw went tight. 'Distinct possibilities,' he bit out.

'You said your country was already unstable,' Olivia continued recklessly. It was so much easier to focus on the politics than what she felt, what she was afraid to feel. 'You said that if people found out Elena was missing it could cause unrest, even a civil war. What if our *marriage* causes one, Aziz?'

'It's a risk I have to take.' His voice was cool, as cool

as she'd ever heard it. 'But I'm aware that it's not a risk you have to take. You don't have to marry me, Olivia. You pointed that out yesterday, and it still holds true today. If the risks are too much for you, then you can back out now. Better now than in an hour, after the vows have been said. Kadarans do not look kindly on divorce.'

He gazed at her evenly, almost indifferently, and with a terrible lurch inside Olivia wondered if he even cared whether she married him. Maybe he had a substitute waiting in the wings. Maybe any woman at all would do.

'And if I backed out now?' she whispered. 'Our wedding is in less than an hour, Aziz.'

'Forty-five minutes, actually,' he answered. 'I confess, it will be difficult to find someone else in that amount of time.'

'I don't want to be just a willing body,' she blurted, her voice breaking. 'I don't want you to be just as happy to choose someone else. I want more than that from a marriage, Aziz. From life.'

He stared at her, his gaze still narrowed. 'What more do you want, Olivia?'

Love. I want you to love me. No, she couldn't say that. She didn't even want to think it. 'All this legal talk just seems very cold,' she said after a moment. 'It makes me realise what I might be missing.'

'Such as?'

'I—I don't know. I sound ridiculous, I know. It's just nerves.' She forced a smile. She was a coward, but she couldn't admit that she wanted more now. She had to focus on what she already had, what she could have. 'I do want this marriage, Aziz. I realised last night how much I want a child, to be a mother again. It won't bring back Daniel, I know, but the thought of having a baby to love… I want that very much.'

For a second, no more, she thought he looked almost disappointed, or maybe even hurt. Or was she just wishing he did? Then he shrugged and said, 'Not to point out the obvious, but you don't need me to have a child, Olivia. You could have one on your own if that's all you really want.'

But it wasn't all she wanted. She didn't just want a baby to love; she wanted a partner to support her. She wanted to be part of a family. 'I want this marriage,' she said firmly. 'And I think you'd be a good father, Aziz.'

His lips curved in a humourless smile. 'Would I? I must admit, I didn't have a great example.'

'Yes, you would. You're fun and kind and easy to—' She swallowed and quickly filled in, 'Like. Besides, lots of people with less than stellar parents have been good ones themselves.'

'Thanks for that vote of confidence.'

Olivia heard a note of bitterness in his voice, and as he turned away she wished she'd been more honest with him. She wished she'd risked her heart a little more and confessed that she wanted so much more than what she'd said. That she wanted a child with him.

And do you remember the last time you risked your heart? You laid it all on the line, confessed all your hope, fear and need, and your father just looked away and asked you to play the damn piano.

Just the memory of that betrayal, and her own reeling reaction, had the power to keep her silent now. It was better this way. She might not feel like it now, but it would be better to keep within the limits of their agreement. To keep herself from wanting it all. *Enough and no more*, just like Aziz had said.

An hour later, it was done.

Aziz jerked off his tie, letting out a weary sigh. He

was married, and within the six weeks dictated by his father's will. He should feel relieved—overjoyed, even—but instead he felt only unsettled and restless, as he had since that confrontation with Olivia.

She'd made it perfectly clear she was only in this marriage to have the child she longed for, nothing else, and certainly not because of any finer feelings she possessed for him.

Feelings he shouldn't even want her to have. He wouldn't beg for love again. He wouldn't debase himself like that, not for anyone. Not even for Olivia. Really, everything had worked out just as he'd wanted. He should be glad now, elated, even.

Not somehow disappointed.

The bathroom door to the bedroom suite they'd been given in a secluded wing of the palace opened and Olivia stood there, dressed in a white silk negligee. It was modest enough, the straps scalloped with lace, but Aziz's mouth still dried and every thought flew from his head.

Every thought but one: his wife was beautiful and he had every intention of making love to her. Tonight.

Now.

He smiled, his gaze sweeping over her lovely, slender form. He could tell just from looking at her, observing her pale face, that she was a little nervous. 'You look beautiful, Olivia.'

'The nightgown is a bit much, isn't it?' she said with a shaky smile. 'Or maybe it's not enough.'

'It's quite enough from my point of view,' he told her, and took a step towards her so he was close enough to slide his hands over her bare shoulders. 'I wouldn't want you any more covered up.' He pressed a kiss to her bare shoulder and she shivered.

'I know we don't need to be—be romantic with one another.'

'Why shouldn't we?' He pressed another kiss to the hollow of her throat and her breath came out in a soft rush.

'Because we…we don't love each other.'

Words that once would have reassured him; now he felt something crystallise inside him, something cold and hard and *hurt*. He didn't like hearing her state it so plainly and he didn't want to think about why. 'Isn't this a kind of love?' he answered. 'Don't dismiss it out of hand, Olivia. Not when you know what I feel for you.' His voice had thickened with need and he pulled her to him, slid his arms around her slender waist, wanting to draw a response from her. Show her just how much she needed and wanted him.

And he felt that need in her answering kiss, in the way her body yielded to his, her curves moulded against him. Aziz eased away just enough to unbutton his shirt, wanting to feel her bare body against his own.

Her gaze roved over his bare chest and her tongue darted out to moisten her lips. A primal triumph surged through him at the obviousness of her desire.

'You should know…it's been a long time for me, Aziz.'

He drew her back towards him, revelling in the way her breasts brushed against his bare chest. 'You don't need to be nervous with me. We can go slowly, Olivia. As slowly as you like.' With a smile, he tugged on her hand and drew her to the bed. The sky was darkening to indigo with violet streaking across the horizon, the minarets and towers of the Old Town silhouetted against the sky.

Olivia lay on her back, her cheeks flushed pale pink, her eyes dark and luminous. The swell of her breasts above the negligee was almost more than Aziz could bear.

Her skin was creamy and perfect, the colour of ivory. He tucked a tendril of hair behind her ear, skimming her cheek with his fingers. He'd always thought her beauty was cold and contained, but seeing her lying here, all flushed and rosy and ready to love, he had to amend his opinion. She was like a flower seeking sunlight, shyly bending towards it. He leaned down and pressed a kiss to her temple. Olivia let out a soft sigh.

Encouraged by her response, Aziz pressed another kiss to her cheek, and then to her lips. Olivia brought her hand up to rest it against Aziz's cheek, and everything in him expanded and ached.

He deepened the kiss, taking his time to explore the softness of her mouth, the fullness of her lips. He slid his hand from her shoulder to her waist, splaying his fingers across her hip, the silk slippery beneath his hand.

Olivia moved restlessly under him, her hand tightening on his cheek, her mouth opening under his. She tangled one leg with his so his fierce arousal was brought into exquisite contact with her thighs and he let out a little groan.

He slid his hand from her waist to her breast, his thumb brushing over its tightened peak as he watched her pupils flare and heard her breathing go shallow. 'You like that?' he asked softly and she nodded.

He bent his mouth to her breast, dampening the silk with his tongue as he took the peak into his mouth. Her hands clutched in his hair. 'Oh…no one's ever…'

'No one?' He drew back, even though he longed to continue, ached to do so much more than that. Still he studied her; her hair was a soft cloud around her face, her face so deliciously flushed, her lips parted. 'You've had lovers, though.'

'Not many. Well, two.' She bit her lip and looked away. 'The boy from high school, of course—'

'In a drunken fumble you barely remember?'

She shrugged. 'And once, when I'd left university, just to see if I could still feel anything.'

His heart twisted inside him. 'And could you?'

She glanced back at him, her eyes heartbreakingly wide. 'No. Not then.'

'And now?' He cupped her breast again through the damp silk and she let out a breathy sigh of pleasure.

'Now, sometimes I wonder if I feel too much.'

An admission that gave him a primal feeling of pleasure, of power. *He'd* made her feel again. He'd been the one to wake her up. 'I think I might need to challenge that assertion,' he murmured and kissed her again, deeply this time, holding nothing back.

He felt her brief hesitation and then she responded, kissing him back with just as much passion, just as much wild, raw feeling that it made him want her even more simply because she wanted him. Olivia's response to him was the most powerful aphrodisiac he'd ever known.

She slid her leg between his, drawing him closer, and he slipped a hand between her thighs, pushing the negligee up so she was bare to the waist.

She stilled, but only for a moment. Then her hands went to his belt buckle, trembling as she fumbled with the clasp. Aziz helped her and then he drew off her clothes as well as his own so they were both wonderfully naked.

'You're perfect,' he murmured. He leaned down and kissed her tummy and then, because he wanted to, *needed* to, he moved lower.

Olivia stilled, her hand still tangled in his hair. 'Aziz…'

'Perfect,' he said again, and kissed her between her thighs.

Olivia felt her body arch up of its own accord, her

breath coming out on a ragged gasp as he kissed her again, spreading her legs open with his hands.

The feelings rushed through her like colours, an intense rainbow of sensation that blurred her thoughts into one single, shining realisation of how much Aziz was showing and giving her.

She felt his mouth on her again and once more she reared up, her breath now coming in shallow pants. She'd never known anything like this, felt anything like this, ever, and it made her want to cry and laugh and sing all at once.

'Aziz,' she choked, because that was the only word she could form. The only thought she could think. She was teetering on a precipice of pleasure, longing to tumble right into it but a little afraid as well. This was so much.

It felt like everything.

'I'm right here,' he said, his voice ragged, and he drew back for one heart-stopping second before he slid inside her, filling her right up.

She'd never felt so close, so connected to another person. Never felt so loved.

This has nothing to do with love.

Her mind made one last, frantic insistence but her body refused to agree; her body sang with the joy of Aziz's touch, everything in her opening up, seeking light.

Aziz began to move, his hands on her hips to encourage her to match his rhythm, which she did instinctively, easily, both of them climbing higher and higher, *reaching…*

And then she did reach that apex of pleasure, all the tightly held parts of herself seeming to loosen and spin away so all she could do was *feel*. Feel every emotion she'd denied for so long. It was so intense and amazing, she cried out, tears starting in her eyes, her body wrapped around Aziz's. In that moment she never wanted to let him go.

As the wave of pleasure subsided to ripples she lay back against the pillows, her skin slick and damp, Aziz's weight a comforting heaviness on top of her. He kissed her forehead and then her lips before rolling off her, one hand still across her stomach, as if he didn't want to let her go.

And she didn't want him to. She thought she'd been changed before, had been opened up, her feelings stirred to life, but she'd had no idea. No clue as to what she'd been missing, what she needed.

She turned to Aziz, wanting to say something of all she felt but unable to put it into words. He must have seen some of it in her eyes, however, for he drew her to him once more, fitting her body so easily to his, and kissed her softly.

Olivia kissed him back, felt his heart beat against hers. Sometimes, she thought, you didn't need words. Sometimes they weren't enough for something that had been so emotional, so incredible.

So wonderful.

She laid her head on Aziz's shoulder and eventually they both slept.

CHAPTER ELEVEN

'A HONEYMOON?' OLIVIA repeated in surprise. 'Is that really…necessary?'

'I'm afraid it is.' Aziz sat across from her at the breakfast table in one of the smaller dining rooms of the palace. Dressed in a navy blue suit, his hair still slightly damp from the shower, it was hard to believe he'd made love to her until nearly dawn last night. Their wedding night.

Now, in the cold light of day, Olivia felt all her old uncertainties return. Once again, Aziz felt like a stranger. And, even though her body burned to remember his touch, her mind scurried for self-protection. She couldn't let him know how much last night had affected her. He'd probably be appalled if he found out.

'Why?' she asked as Aziz poured them both coffee.

'It's best if we both stay out of sight for a few days. My marriage has been announced, but not the name of my bride.'

'But everyone will assume—'

'It's Elena. Yes, I know.' He gave her a rather grim smile. 'This is going to a very delicate diplomatic manoeuvre.'

'So how do you intend to announce it?'

'I want to speak to Khalil first and arrange for Elena's release.'

'You make it sound easy.'

'No, just necessary. Now that I'm married he has no reason to keep her. I hope he'll be able to see sense and put aside this desire for revenge.'

'Maybe it's not revenge motivating him,' Olivia said slowly, and Aziz swung his gaze back to her.

'What, then?'

'Maybe, like you, he wants to redeem the past. You were both treated badly by Hashem, in different ways.'

Aziz felt himself bristle. 'He was banished because he was not Hashem's son.'

'But he thought he was, and that had to have hurt him terribly. He lost everything he ever knew, Aziz, and he was just a little boy.'

'He lived a life of luxury in America,' he said stiffly. 'I'm sorry if I can't feel sorry for him.'

'I'm not asking you to feel sorry for him,' Olivia answered after a moment. 'I don't care about Khalil, to be honest. But…' She let out a soft breath. 'I care about how he affects you. Maybe there is a way to put this conflict to rest, to find peace, not just for Kadar but for you and Khalil.'

He let out a hard laugh. 'Peace with Khalil? Never.'

'It's not like you to be so bitter or unforgiving, Aziz,' she protested.

'You don't know—'

'What? Tell me.' She held her breath, wanting him to share something of himself. Wanting to understand him, to help him.

Because she was falling in love with him. And she didn't know how to stop.

Her fingers gripped her fork and she laid it down on the table; she couldn't eat anything anyway.

'Nothing,' Aziz said, his tone final. 'It doesn't matter.

In any case, we don't need to talk politics now. We can enjoy ourselves, for a few days, at least.'

She nodded, knowing she needed to let it go, at least for now. 'Where are we going?'

'To another royal palace, this one on the coast. It's in a very remote and beautiful spot. I'm sure you'll love it.'

'I don't have any clothes or cosmetics.'

'Everything you need will be provided.' He hesitated, his face so very bland. 'Unless you wish to return to Paris for some reason? The terms of our agreement allow—'

'I don't,' she said, hating the thought of that legal document that defined their marriage in such businesslike terms. 'Although I probably should at some point. I'd like to get my things.'

'Of course. You can go back whenever you like, assuming you have no royal duties.'

She stared at him, half-wanting to ask him if he'd miss her, or if he wanted her to go. Maybe he'd rather have her out of the way. She had no idea what he felt, and it seemed absurd to think he'd feel anything, when they'd been no more than employer and employee for six years. This relationship, this marriage, was so very new and strange.

'It's settled, then.' Aziz rose from the table. 'I'll meet you in the grand foyer in an hour. We'll travel to the coast by helicopter. There's a helipad at the back of the palace.'

She nodded, her mind still whirling, and Aziz strode from the room.

An hour later they were in a helicopter high above the desert, the Arabian Sea jewel-bright in the distance and sparkling with sunlight.

Aziz had told her it would only take an hour to get to the palace, and Olivia spent the time gazing out of the window, entranced by the starkly beautiful scenery. The desert terrain was scattered with huge, black boulders, like misshapen marbles tossed from a giant's hand. As they drew closer to the sea, the craggy, forbidding coastline came into view. The palace, Aziz had said, was hidden in its own private cove, inaccessible except by helicopter or boat.

As they landed, the sight of the palace took her breath away. Made of the same mellow, golden brick as the palace in Siyad, this coastal retreat was still completely different, built right into the rock, its elegant towers pointing towards the sky.

'It's quite something,' Aziz said with a small smile. 'I've only been here once before myself.'

Olivia followed him from the helicopter towards the steps cut into the cliff side that curved steeply up to the palace. 'Why only once?'

Aziz shrugged. 'As you know, I spent as little time in Kadar as possible. I think we went here once for a family holiday—my father's birthday, if I remember.' He sounded indifferent, as if he barely remembered when or why he'd been, but Olivia still wondered.

'Tell me about your father,' she said quietly and, even though he was several steps ahead of her, Olivia *felt* him stiffen.

'Why on earth would I want to talk about him?' he answered after a pause.

Olivia waited until they'd reached the top of the cliff-side steps, the palace's ornate wooden doors in front of them. 'Because I know your relationship with him was a troubled one, and it affects you even now. I want to understand.'

'There's nothing to understand.' Aziz turned to open the doors and then began greeting the staff who were lined up in the mosaic-tiled foyer.

Olivia followed him, murmuring her own greetings,

and then they were shown to their private quarters, a beautiful suite of rooms with balconies overlooking a garden with cascading pools, the sea visible beyond. She decided to let the personal questions go for now. There would be time later, she hoped, to get Aziz to open up to her.

'This is amazing,' she said as she stood on a balcony, gazing out at the magnificent view. 'I can hardly believe I'm here.'

Aziz stood in the doorway, the latticed shutters open to the wind and sun. 'It's been a whirlwind few days.'

'Yes.' In the space of just seventy-two hours she'd gone from impersonating a queen to marrying a Sheikh. No wonder her head was still spinning.

Her hands curved around the stone railing, her gaze still fixed on the sea shimmering under the noonday sun. She wanted to tell Aziz something of what was in her heart. She wanted to tell him that in the space of just a few days he'd changed her. And, even though it was scary, she was glad she'd changed, grateful that he'd opened her up.

And she wanted to change him too, to show him that you could risk your heart again, that love was worth it. But how could she explain any of that when she wasn't even sure if she believed it? When just the thought of telling him, never mind living it out, scared her senseless?

Why couldn't she just be satisfied with what Aziz had offered? *Enough and no more.* He didn't want to go deeper with her, even if she now thought she might want to. She'd already told him her secrets; he had no call to tell her his.

You haven't told him everything. No, she hadn't gone into much detail about those awful, endless years after she'd given up Daniel. Hadn't admitted just how low she'd sunk, how she hadn't thought she'd ever crawl out of that dark, dark hole. Hadn't admitted how it wasn't just losing

Daniel but losing her parents', and especially her father's, trust that had made her retreat into isolated numbness.

And he probably didn't want to hear it all now.

He came to stand behind her and rested his hands lightly on her shoulders. 'How about a swim?'

She glanced down at the cascading pools and then smiled up at him. *Enough.* She'd let this, him, be enough. 'That sounds good.'

They spent three days at the coastal palace, chatting and laughing, swimming and making love. With every day she spent in Aziz's company, every hour, Olivia knew she was falling deeper and deeper in love with him. She also knew he wasn't falling in love with her.

She saw how, even when he was right there with her, he kept some part of himself removed. Remote. Even when she lay in his arms, when he kissed her, when he buried himself inside her, he held something back.

And as the days passed she knew with an utter certainty that she wanted that part, wanted to reach all of him. Love all of him. Even if it was scary. Even if it hurt.

She just didn't know how to *begin.*

'I love hearing you laugh,' Aziz said as they lay on the sun-warmed tiles by the main pool's waterfall one afternoon, another pool shimmering below them. 'It makes me realise how little I heard it in Paris. How sad you seemed, but I don't think I quite realised it then.'

Olivia rolled onto her stomach. 'Why should you have? I was just your housekeeper.'

'And you're my wife now.' He stroked her cheek and Olivia took a deep breath. For the last three days she'd been telling herself that she shouldn't push, yet now she couldn't keep herself from it. She wanted to know more about this man she cared about. This man she loved.

'Aziz, will you tell me more about yourself? About your past and your childhood and what made you leave Kadar?'

His fingers stilled on her cheek then he dropped his hand and turned onto his back, staring up at the cloudless blue sky. Olivia waited, hoping he might tell her at least a little.

'There's not all that much to tell, really,' he said after an endless moment. His voice sounded almost disinterested, but Olivia knew now how Aziz hid himself from her and from everyone with a light tone, a raised eyebrow, a teasing smile. His mask.

'Everyone has something to tell,' she answered, matching his light tone. Deliberately she reached out and skimmed one hand along his bare chest, running her fingertips through the water droplets that beaded there. Touching him still felt a little strange, and filled her with wonder. She liked it and wanted it to become familiar, easy. Natural. 'And, whatever your story is,' she continued, running her fingertip along the defined muscles of his abdomen, 'I want to hear it.'

Aziz trapped her hand against his stomach and twisted to look up at her with a wicked smile. 'Are you sure you wouldn't rather do something else instead?'

'*Aziz.*'

'You want to hear me blather on about my childhood?' He moved her hand a little lower. 'I'd like to hear you moan with pleasure.'

She flushed, desire already coursing through her veins in a molten river. She wanted that too, just as much.

Almost.

'Aziz, I'm serious.'

'So am I.' But he let go of her hand with a sigh and stared up at the sky once more. 'So, what do you want to know? My favourite subject in school? My hobbies? I liked maths and making paper aeroplanes.'

'That's a start, I suppose,' Olivia answered with a little smile. 'I could have guessed the maths, considering what a financial whiz you are now. The paper aeroplanes are a bit of a surprise.'

'I used to drive my mother mad, with all the crumpled sheets of paper lying around.'

'Were you very close to your mother?'

He shrugged, the movement easy, yet his face had gone still, blank. Olivia sighed.

'Do you not want to tell me *anything*, Aziz?'

'I thought,' he said after a moment, 'That wasn't the kind of relationship we were meant to have.'

Stung, she blinked a few times, forcing the hurt back. He was right, she knew that. She was the one who had changed, not him. 'I told you my secrets.'

He gazed at her, his face bland, inscrutable. 'Do you regret it?'

'No, I don't. It felt good to open up like that. Scary and surprising, but good.' She hesitated, then made herself add, 'Maybe you'd find it was too.'

'Cathartic soul-baring? Hmm, I'm not so sure.' He was back to being teasing, masking the evasion with a playful smile. 'I can think of a few other things I'd like to do,' he added, and reached out with one hand to toy suggestively with the strap of her swimming costume.

Olivia pulled away slightly. 'I'm not asking for your deepest secrets,' she said, trying to sound as casual as he did. She had a feeling she hadn't quite managed it. 'I just want to know you a little better. We are married, after all.'

Aziz was silent for a moment; he slid one hand up and down her arm almost absently, his brow furrowed. 'All right,' he finally said. 'What is it you wanted to know?

Was I close to my mother? Yes, as a small child. But when we moved to the palace she withdrew more and more from everyone, even me, and then I hardly saw her after I went away to school.' He flipped onto his stomach and reached for her again. 'Now, let's get back to the more important issue…'

And, with a little laugh, Olivia let him draw her towards him. She didn't think she'd get much farther with Aziz's confidences just then, and in any case she had neither the willpower nor the desire to resist him any longer.

Later, the shuttered windows open to the sun setting over the Arabian Sea turning the placid water to gold, they lay on the huge canopied bed, legs entwined, heart rates slowing.

A sleepy satisfaction was stealing through Olivia, making her feel almost boneless. Aziz pressed a hand to her flat stomach.

'Do you think we made a little prince or princess already?' he asked in a lazy murmur, and pressed a kiss to her navel.

Olivia's insides jolted with surprise; she hadn't even been thinking about babies since Aziz had first made love to her, which was a bit ridiculous, considering how she'd made it her main reason to marry him.

Not quite your main reason.

She might have presented it to him as her main reason, so she wouldn't scare him off, but, cocooned in the intimacy of a sleepy afternoon's love-making, Olivia knew she hadn't agreed to marry Aziz just for the sake of a child, or for the promise of companionship or sex.

She'd married him because she'd been falling in love with him, had been falling in love with him since she'd first come to Kadar—or perhaps even before then.

Maybe she'd been fooling herself all along. Maybe Aziz had been waking her up slowly with his gentle teasing and easy smiles. It had taken coming to Kadar and moving right out of her comfort zone, out of herself, to bring her fully to life. To make her realise she loved him.

'What are you thinking about?' Aziz asked as he kissed his way up her belly. Olivia glanced down at his tousled ink-dark hair, saw his glinting eyes, his teasing smile. She knew he didn't want to hear what she'd been really thinking about. He'd be horrified if he knew just how much she felt for him.

'Nothing too serious,' she said lightly and touched his hair.

'You look awfully serious,' Aziz answered. He pressed one last kiss to her stomach and then rolled onto his back, his hand linked loosely with hers.

Olivia gazed down at their joined hands and knew she couldn't keep from pushing to know more about him, at least a little. 'I was thinking about you, Aziz.' She smiled, although it felt wobbly. 'I was imagining you running through the halls of the palace, paper aeroplanes whizzing through the air.'

He gave her a small smile back, but Olivia saw his expression had turned wary.

'Perhaps our son, or our daughter, for that matter, will do the same.'

Was he reminding her why she was here at all? Olivia wondered. For the sake of a child. Suddenly her admission that she was only marrying him so she could be a mother again seemed incredibly cold. She wanted to tell Aziz she didn't feel that way any more, maybe had never even felt that way, but somehow the words wouldn't come.

'Maybe,' she answered, even though it seemed no more than a distant dream. She could be pregnant, she reminded herself. They hadn't used protection and her cycle was irregular. But she didn't want to think about a baby just now. She wanted to think about Aziz.

'You said you were close to your mother,' she began, and Aziz rolled into a sitting position.

'Why are you digging, Olivia?' he asked as he reached for his shirt.

'Digging? Is that what it feels like? I just want to know—'

'Why? What difference does it make? It's a little late for second thoughts.'

'*Second thoughts?* I'm not having second thoughts.'

'If you're worried about what kind of father I'll make,' Aziz clarified with a shrug, as if this conversation was already boring him. Olivia watched him slip on his shorts. He raked a hand through his hair and reached for his watch.

'Aziz,' she said slowly, 'This has nothing to do with what kind of father you'll make. I want to know about you for your sake, and mine. Because you're my husband and, regardless of what we agreed or signed, we're married and we have a relationship that is meant to last a lifetime.' She took a breath and ploughed on. 'Are you going to push me away for ever?'

'I wasn't aware you wanted to get closer.'

Her heart seemed to still and then beat harder. 'And if I did?' she asked after a moment.

Aziz's back was to her, so she couldn't see his face—not that she'd be able to tell what he was thinking or feeling if she could see it. He was, Olivia knew, amazingly adept at hiding his feelings. Just as she'd once been.

Aziz remained with his back to Olivia. He didn't know what to say to her, had no idea what she wanted from him. He'd been evading her questions all day, unwilling to open up, as she now seemed to want him to do. *And for what?* She'd made it clear what she wanted from him and this marriage.

A child. Nothing more.

'I don't really see the purpose of some kind of heart-to-heart,' he finally said, his back still to her. 'We agreed we didn't really want to know each other that way.'

'We also agreed that everything was up for discussion,' Olivia reminded him. 'Has that changed?'

'No,' Aziz answered after a moment. He turned around to see Olivia sitting cross-legged in the middle of the bed, her hair, now almost back to its caramel colour, spilling over her shoulders. She had a sheet wrapped around her and her skin was creamy and flushed pink. She looked, Aziz thought, utterly beautiful and happier than he'd ever seen her before, despite the faint shadows in her eyes. Shadows he suspected he was putting there with his reticence.

He sat on the edge of the bed and stared down at the rumpled sheets.

'My father,' he said slowly, each word emerging from his tightened throat with effort, 'Always resented me and the fact that he needed me as his heir.'

'Because of Khalil?' she asked softly.

His throat went tighter as he nodded. 'He always loved him. Always preferred him.'

'But he banished him.'

'I know, and he hated that he'd had to do it. Khalil was his adored first son, the pet of the palace, of the whole damn country—' He broke off, hearing how ragged his voice had sounded, feeling his heart start to thud, the old anger and bitterness rising up inside him in an unstoppable tide.

He hadn't wanted to rake all this up, to remember it. Being back in Kadar was hard enough without trawling through all the awful memories of his childhood. Yet now that he'd started he found he couldn't stop. He didn't even want to stop.

He drew his hand away from Olivia's and rose from the bed, his back to her. 'You want to know about me, Olivia? Fine, here's the unfiltered version: my father hated me. *Hated* me, from the moment I entered the palace, or maybe even before.'

He took a shuddering breath, let it out slowly. 'Although, I suppose he didn't care enough to hate me before he had to make me his heir. But when he did, he resented me for it. Resented the fact that he needed me, so he made my life a complete misery.'

He heard how his voice shook and self-loathing poured through him, as corrosive as acid. He hated remembering this. Talking about it was even worse and yet, even though he'd spent most of his life pretending his childhood hadn't happened, hiding himself and all his fears and deficiencies from everyone, now he felt a compulsion to come clean.

It was like that impulse you had to throw yourself off a bridge or under a train, he thought darkly. The death instinct, Freud called it, and he was feeling it now.

Perversely, stupidly, he wanted to tell Olivia everything. He just didn't think he could bear the look he'd see on her face when he did.

Right now, however, when he risked a glance towards her sitting there on the bed, she looked calm. 'How old were you when you became the heir?' she asked.

'Four.'

'Oh, Aziz.' Her voice and face both softened with a sympathy he couldn't stand. It felt like pity. 'Tell me about it,' she entreated, her voice so soft and sad it wound around him with its silken strands, made him trapped, furious and desperate.

'You really want to know all the ugly, pathetic details? We were despised, my mother and I. Loathed and ridiculed from the moment we stepped through those hallowed doors—by my father, by the palace staff, by everyone. It just about killed my mother. She was a village girl, chosen to be the Sheikh's mistress with no say in the matter. She'd never wanted to be queen.'

'*Aziz,*' Olivia whispered, but he barely heard her. Now that he'd started, he didn't think he could stop, not until it was all out, every last, terrible detail.

'At first it was just little things—forgetting to bow or give her the respect she deserved as queen. She ignored it, because it seemed easier. Safer. Then, encouraged by my father, people grew bold, taunting her and me. Tripping us as we walked by. Starting rumours in the palace, in the city bazaar. My father went along with it all.' Aziz swallowed, the taste of acid on his tongue, churning in his stomach. 'He made a mockery of us both. My mother stopped making any public appearances. She lived in her private rooms, terrified that she would be banished like Khalil. Just as I was terrified.' He swallowed, his throat working, his breath coming in pants, before he calmed himself by sheer force of will.

When he spoke again, his voice was flat, dispassionate. 'My father lived to show everyone how deficient I was in every respect. He'd drag me into his chambers, ridicule me in front of all his cabinet members.' And still he'd tried to please him. He'd spent hours memorising anything his father might quiz him on: his times tables, facts about Kadaran history, every law of the Kadaran constitution. If he failed on one point, his father branded him a failure. Slapped his face and told him to get out.

'Oh, Aziz,' she said, 'I'm so sorry.'

'You know the worst part?' he said in a low voice, unable to look at her now. 'I still loved him. Why, God only knows. But I loved him and—' He stopped, hating that he was telling her this. That he *needed* to tell her this. 'I wanted him to love me. I did everything I could, every single thing, to try and make him love me.' His voice choked and he swore, turning furiously away from her. 'I even asked him once. I asked him, point-blank, why he didn't love me.' He shook his head, the memory twenty years old, yet still possessing the power to make him feel like that desperate, cringing boy. 'Do you know what he said?'

'No,' Olivia said, her voice quiet and sad.

Aziz stared blindly out of the window. 'He said, "why would I?"' He let out a defeated, weary laugh. 'I've never been able to answer that question.'

'I can answer it, Aziz,' Olivia whispered and he realised just how pathetic he must sound, whinging about how no one loved him.

'Not another one of your pep talks, please,' he said, trying to keep his voice light, to reassemble his armour. The Gentleman Playboy in full force. 'It's ancient history now anyway.'

'It still matters.'

'Well, yes, because it's affected my choices now. That's why you don't need to worry that I'll fall in love with you, Olivia.' He forced himself to smile at her, as if this was actually reassurance he wanted to offer. 'I'm not interested in wearing my heart on my sleeve ever again.'

'I know you're not,' she said quietly. 'But just because your father rejected you doesn't mean other people will.'

'Not a risk worth taking, in my opinion. And not in yours either, I thought.' He spoke sharply, reminding himself as well as her just what the terms of their marriage were—and why.

Because you could never convince someone to love you, no matter what you did. Better not to try. Not then and not now.

Olivia drew her knees up to her chest, circling them with her slender arms. 'And the Gentleman Playboy,' she said after a moment. 'Where did that come from?'

He tensed. 'What do you mean?'

'How did a little boy longing for love from his father became the playboy of Europe?'

He flinched at her assessment, hating how she'd put it into words. That was who he'd been, who he still was.

'When I was fifteen, I discovered women.' He raised his eyebrows, forced another teasing smile. 'My father's mistress, actually. She seduced me and at first I went along with it just to lash out at him. Then I realised I could please women, and focused on that rather than the impossible task of trying to please my father.' He'd meant to sound light but it just came out bitter.

'I see,' she said quietly, and he knew she did. She saw far, far too much.

'I don't know why we're talking about this.'

'Because I want to know you. Understand you.'

'Satisfied?' he demanded, his voice ringing out, and she just looked at him. He saw pity on her face, in the dark eyes and turned-down mouth, and he hated it.

He swung away from her, stalking to the window, his hands curling around the sun-warmed stone as he stared out at the sky that had darkened to deep indigo.

'So,' he finally managed, and his voice sounded a little

more like his usual self, the self he'd chosen to be. 'You really felt better after that kind of confessional?'

She laughed softly, sadly. 'Not right away. Mostly I felt shell-shocked and emotionally exhausted.' He heard the whisper of sheets as she rose from the bed and came to stand behind him. She rested a hand on his shoulder. 'But in time, Aziz, I hope you'll feel better. Stronger. And I hope you'll be glad you told me.'

He doubted it. Already he was regretting having revealed so much, shown so much weakness.

'Aziz,' she murmured, and slid her arms around his waist, drawing her gently back to him. His back collided with her bare softness, but in that moment he didn't feel desire.

He felt something deeper, something more overwhelming; his throat tightened and his eyes stung. He reached for her hand, not even knowing what he felt, only that he didn't want her to leave him then.

Or ever.

'Aziz,' Olivia said again softly, her arms still around him, her fingers threaded through his. 'Aziz, I know you might not think you want to hear—'

A knock sounded on the door and Olivia fell silent. With a sad little sigh, she slipped away from him and reached for a robe.

Aziz turned, waiting until she'd belted it and was covered before saying in a clipped voice, 'Come in.'

To his surprise, it was Malik. He didn't look at Olivia, but kept his rather grim gaze trained on Aziz.

'Aziz, we've received a message from Khalil. He wishes to speak with you.'

Stunned, for a few seconds, he could only stare. 'Speak with me?'

'He is in Siyad and can come here by helicopter in an hour.'

An hour. Aziz's mind spun with this new revelation as well as everything that had just happened between him and Olivia.

'You'll speak to him?' Malik confirmed, and he nodded.

'Yes. Prepare one of the rooms downstairs for our meeting, please.'

Malik left and he turned to glance at Olivia; he saw she looked white-faced and apprehensive. He probably looked the same. He certainly felt it. He had no idea what Khalil wanted to say to him; he doubted his former half-brother was coming to renounce his claim. As for anything between him and Olivia...

'What do you want me to do?' Olivia asked, and he almost reached for her hand, almost asked her to stay with him, because he needed her. Needed both her strength and her sympathy, her understanding and compassion.

And he didn't want to need her. Didn't want to need anyone, to open himself up to that weakness.

And yet he knew it was already too late. He'd been trying to protect his heart and he'd failed. He loved her. He loved her so much it hurt.

He imagined asking Olivia if she loved him and having her say the same words his father had once said to him.

Why would I?

She'd phrase it more nicely, of course. She might even apologise. But she'd make it clear that she didn't love him, couldn't love him, and there was no way in hell he was ever going to let himself in for that kind of rejection and pain again.

'Just wait here,' he said and left the room.

CHAPTER TWELVE

AZIZ WALKED AWAY from Olivia, still reeling from everything he'd confessed and felt. And now Khalil was coming here. With that coming on the heels of his conversation with Olivia, he felt as if his nerve-endings had been scraped raw.

'This could be a good thing,' Malik said quietly, and Aziz shrugged.

'Or he could be declaring his intentions.' Khalil might demand he call the referendum. No matter that he'd fulfilled the terms of his father's will; the people still supported Khalil, or at least most of them, and Khalil could argue that Aziz should let the people decide.

And maybe he should. Maybe clinging onto a title nobody wanted him to have was foolish. He'd never earned his father's love; why did he think he could earn his country's?

Yet Olivia believed he could. The memory strengthened his resolve. He wasn't going to give it all away now.

Half an hour later, showered and dressed in a pair of dark trousers and a button-down shirt, Aziz prowled the elegant confines of one of the palace's smaller receiving rooms. He could have stood on ceremony as ruling Sheikh and been seated on a throne of gold and silver but such petty tactics seemed both obvious and pathetic. He was above them, he hoped.

He hadn't spoken or seen Olivia since Malik had entered the bedroom. He just thought of her, remembering how she'd drawn him against her, her arms around him, how good he'd felt...

He knew she'd been going to tell him something. Something he probably didn't want to hear, because it would just make him love her more.

Aziz whirled around, stalked the length of the room. He loved her, but he was utterly afraid to tell her. If that made him a coward, then so be it. He couldn't risk offering his heart again. Couldn't bear to see the look on her face as she tried to let him down gently, reminded him of their awful arrangement...

It was better this way, he told himself. Better to face Khalil alone, to keep the feelings in. Eventually they would fade. He'd learn not to feel so much for her.

A thought which felt like an even worse agony.

In the distance he heard the hectic whirring of a helicopter's blades and his gaze met Malik's steady one.

'Why don't you meet him, Malik? I'll wait here.'

The older man nodded and Aziz resumed pacing as he waited for the man he'd once thought was his half-brother to arrive.

Five seemingly endless minutes later, a knock sounded on the door. Aziz turned around, his heart thudding. 'Enter.'

The door opened and Khalil stood there, Malik behind him.

Aziz stared at the man he had no blood relation to, yet whose life had been twined with his since birth. Khalil stood tall and proud, but without any anger in his eyes.

Aziz had expected a rebellious firebrand, but Khalil seemed too calm and composed for that.

He nodded tersely. 'Come in.' Khalil took a step forward and Aziz glanced at Malik. 'You may leave us.'

His aide nodded and closed the doors behind Khalil, leaving the two men alone. Neither of them spoke for a long, taut moment.

Finally Aziz broke the silence. 'I forgot how still and quiet you can be.'

Khalil arched an eyebrow. 'You remember me?'

'I remember meeting you when I was four.'

'That was weeks before Hashem banished me.'

'Was it?' The memories were blurred in Aziz's mind. 'I suppose it was.' Enough reminiscing, he thought with a sudden surge of impatient anger. 'Why are you here, Khalil? What have you done with Queen Elena?'

'She is safe.'

'Where is she?' Aziz's voice came out like the crack of a whip. 'Don't you realise you could face imprisonment for kidnapping?'

'Elena won't press charges.'

Aziz grimaced. 'Did you terrify her into agreeing to that? What did you threaten—?'

'Enough, Aziz.' Khalil held up one hand. 'I regret my actions now.'

Aziz bared his teeth in a smile. 'I'm afraid that's not quite good enough for me.'

'I wouldn't expect it to be. We have been enemies a long time.'

'You still haven't told me where Elena is.'

'She is waiting for me in Siyad.' Khalil paused, his expression still so very composed. 'We're married, Aziz.'

Aziz's breath came out in a rush. 'You forced her!'

'It was not forced.'

Aziz didn't speak for a moment. So Elena had changed sides, abandoned him. Could he really be surprised? He'd abandoned her too, after all. 'Why did she agree?' he finally asked, his voice flat and hard. 'Did she actually believe your claim?'

'She did, as I did. All my decisions have been based on believing I was the rightful heir to Kadar's throne.'

'Even though you have no blood relation to my father.'

'I thought I did.'

Aziz stared at him, utterly nonplussed. 'What?'

'I thought I did,' Khalil repeated, his voice a low throb. 'My whole life, I thought Hashem had banished me simply because he preferred your mother. Preferred you.'

Aziz let out a choked laugh of disbelief. *Preferred him?* Did Khalil really have no idea how absurd a notion that was? 'And then what happened?' he asked.

'I found out two days ago that Hashem wasn't my father. My mother had an affair with one of the palace guards.'

Aziz stared at Khalil, saw how his jaw bunched and his throat worked. It must have been, he realised, a hard fact to accept. 'How did you learn of this?'

'My mother's sister told me. She kept it from me for many years because she didn't want to tarnish my mother's memory. But when she saw that I'd—that I'd found Elena, she thought maybe I'd changed enough to hear it. To accept it.'

'Found Elena,' Aziz repeated neutrally. 'What does that mean, exactly, Khalil?'

'We love each other.'

He swung away, jammed his hands in the pockets of his trousers. 'I see.'

'Elena has made me realise how much more there is to this life than cold, hard ambition. My whole existence was oriented towards reclaiming my birthright. Every decision, every choice—' Khalil broke off. 'Aziz, I accept the throne is not mine. It was never mine. I'm renouncing my claim.'

Aziz knew he should feel something: joy; relief; satisfaction *something*. He felt nothing at all. He turned back, stared at Khalil and felt empty. 'You really think it's that simple?' he finally asked evenly. 'You renounce your claim and everything becomes easy?'

'No,' Khalil answered. 'Nothing about this is easy.'

'More than half the country supports you,' Aziz stated. 'If we called the referendum right now, you would still win, whether you had a claim or not.'

'Maybe,' Khalil allowed. 'But I've been travelling through the desert for six months, rallying support. You haven't even been in Kadar.'

Although Khalil spoke neutrally, Aziz still felt the accusation, even the contempt. 'So the Gentleman Playboy has been carousing through Europe?' he proposed cynically. 'Is that what you think?'

'Tell me differently.'

'Why should I? I don't owe you anything, not even an explanation.'

'No, I don't suppose you do.' Khalil regarded him evenly. 'I'm sorry,' he said after a moment, 'For kidnapping Elena and making things harder for you.'

'And I should just accept your apology?' Aziz answered incredulously.

'No,' Khalil answered, 'You probably shouldn't. But I don't know what else to do. I want to make this right, Aziz. You are the rightful Sheikh. I've spent months—hell, a lifetime—acting otherwise. But I recognise it now and my hope is that we can work together for the sake of

Kadar.' He paused, his gaze shuttered. 'But I'll understand if you feel we can't.'

Olivia's words, her soft voice, echoed through him. *I care about he affects you. Maybe there is a way to put this conflict to rest, to find peace, not just for Kadar but for you and Khalil.*

It felt impossible, yet Olivia believed it could be so. She believed in *him*, that he might be strong enough to move beyond the past. His throat was thick with emotion as he bit out, 'My life was hell because of you.'

Khalil blinked, clearly surprised. '*Your* life was hell? I spent three years in the desert being whipped like a dog.'

'What?' Aziz gaped at him. 'You went to America—'

'Only after my aunt found me. Hashem had me sent to the desert, to my mother's tribe. The sheikh hated me and he let me know it every day of my life.'

Just as Hashem had done to him. Aziz's mind spun with his new information. 'I'm sorry,' he said after a moment, knowing anything he said now would be inadequate. 'I didn't know.'

Khalil let out a hard laugh. 'You thought I was living the high life in America?'

'You've assumed I was living like a spoilt prince.'

'Hashem *chose* you,' Khalil said emphatically. 'Over me. He chose you, he made you his heir, so—'

'So what do I have to complain about?' Aziz filled in. 'Poor little playboy? Maybe I am.' He swung away once more, hating that he was raking this all up *again*. 'Maybe I am,' he repeated quietly, and neither of them spoke for another long, tense minute.

Finally Khalil broke the silence. 'Why was your life hell, Aziz?'

'My father might have banished you from the palace,' Aziz said after a moment, 'But he never banished you from his heart. He loved you, Khalil.' He turned around, realising how Khalil needed to hear this. To know it. 'He always loved you. He banished you, I suppose, because he felt he had no choice, but in his mind and heart you were his real son. Not me.'

Khalil's jaw bunched and he blinked rapidly. 'He had a funny way of showing it.'

Aziz nodded; his anger was leaving him in a rush, leaving him only sad and weary. 'Yes, I suppose he did.'

'You actually expect me to believe Hashem loved me and still threw me to a man like Abdul-Hafiz? Let me be beaten and starved and shamed for three years?'

'I'm not defending his actions,' Aziz answered. 'I don't know why he did what he did. Maybe anger won out over love. Maybe he didn't know how to deal with his disappointment. Maybe he was just what he's always seemed to me—a cruel, petty, sadistic bastard.'

'Maybe he was,' Khalil agreed after a moment. 'But if he really loved me so much,' he continued in a low voice, 'He could have accepted me. Found a place for me.'

'I know. Trust me, I know. Coming to the palace and being made his heir was the worst thing that ever happened to me.'

Khalil shook his head slowly. 'Whenever I thought of you, I pictured you as a spoilt little prince being fawned over by everyone, given your every heart's desire.'

Aziz let out a hollow laugh. 'That was far, far from the truth.'

Khalil nodded again. 'So we both suffered.'

'Yes. Hashem has a lot to answer for.'

'And he's not here to pay the price. We are.' They were both silent, but Aziz felt the tension between them had eased a little. He had no idea what kind of relationship, if any, he could have with Khalil, but he knew this man was no longer his enemy.

Olivia had helped him to see that now, he realised. Olivia had changed him, made him want to move on. *Made him love.*

'Let me help you,' Khalil said quietly. 'Let me help our country. Together we can repair the damage our father caused to Kadar's very fabric. We can unite the people—'

Aziz eyed him with a weary scepticism coupled with the most fragile hope. 'How?'

'By telling the truth. By being united ourselves. You are the rightful Sheikh, Aziz, and I accept that.'

'Even if you don't want to.'

'I do not have the liberty to indulge my desires. Accepting I do not have any right to the throne is difficult. I am still coming to terms with it.'

'And what of Elena?'

'We love each other. She has accepted I will not be Sheikh, although I am still ruler of my mother's tribe, and as such I give my obeisance to you.'

To Aziz's shock Khalil sank to one knee, his head bowed. Aziz's eyes stung and he blinked rapidly.

'Get up,' he said, his voice choked. 'I've never stood on ceremony.'

Khalil rose slowly, his gaze steady. 'People like you, Aziz. You have charmed most of Europe. You can win the affection of the people of Kadar.'

'Thank you for your vote of confidence.' Except, Aziz acknowledged, he'd won the love of people by not being himself. By play-acting a role he was already tired of. *And when people learned the truth...*

Olivia knew the truth. He'd spilled his sad, sorry secrets to her and she was still here, still supporting him.

Loving him?

Was that what she'd been going to tell him? Could he dare believe that she felt even a little for him what he felt for her?

Could he risk baring his heart to another person, begging someone to love him back?

Aziz blinked the questions back. 'You must have heard, I've married myself,' he told Khalil.

'Yes.'

'Since it's not Elena, the people may have trouble accepting my bride.'

'Then it is up to you to show them how capable she is.'

And Olivia was certainly that. She was calm, strong and dignified, yet with so much heart and warmth. He hadn't seen it at first, not when she'd just been his cool, capable housekeeper. But he saw it now and he felt his heart swell with pride. She would, he thought, make an excellent queen.

'You can do this,' Khalil said quietly. 'You can do it on your own, but it would be my honour to help you.'

Aziz stared at Khalil for a long moment, his thoughts whirling through his mind like leaves in a storm. Then slowly he nodded and reached out to shake the other man's hand.

The past was, at least in part, forgiven. Healed. He had Olivia to thank for it; he knew that. Olivia had helped him and healed him in so many ways.

He needed to tell her that, needed to tell her so much. If only he could find the courage.

Two hours had passed since Aziz had left their bedroom and the sky was inky-black and spangled with stars. Olivia had been staring at it through the window, the shutters thrown open to the night, her mind first blank and paralyzed, then seething with questions and fears, and back again.

At some point she dressed, and Mada brought food in that she couldn't eat. She paced the room restlessly and then picked at a salad, nearly threw it up and went back to the bed, sitting on its edge as she clutched a pillow to her chest.

In her mind she went over that last exchange with Aziz. He'd looked so cold, so closed. She'd wanted to be with him, to share this with him and support him in whatever happened with Khalil, but he hadn't wanted her. That had been all too painfully obvious.

She clutched the pillow hard, felt the first threat of tears. Maybe she should just give up. Admit defeat. Accept what Aziz was offering, or even try to live apart if it would hurt too much.

Or you could tell him you love him.

The thought flooded her with terror. What would happen if he told her he didn't love her? If he looked appalled or horrified? She might slide into the kind of endless despair she'd felt after losing Daniel. Losing Aziz, she knew with heart-sickening clarity, would be just as painful.

She heard the snick of the door opening and closing and Olivia glanced up, the pillow still clutched to her chest.

Aziz stood there, his expression impossible to read. Olivia swallowed hard.

'What happened?' she managed in a whisper and Aziz walked slowly into the room. He turned to gaze out of the window, his back to her.

'Khalil has renounced his claim.'

'Renounced—?' Olivia stopped and stared at Aziz

who was still facing away from her. 'But that's good news, isn't it?' she asked uncertainly because he didn't seem happy.

'Very good news.' Aziz's voice was flat. 'Apparently he'd always believed he was the rightful heir. He didn't think his mother had ever been unfaithful to my father.'

'And he learned…'

'The truth. Yesterday. His aunt told him. He's officially withdrawing his claim. There will be no war, no referendum. He wants to support my rule, help heal our country.' He stated all this so matter-of-factly, his back still to her.

Olivia stared at him in confusion and then with a terrible, dawning realisation: his throne was essentially secure. If he wanted to, he could end their marriage. After all, he'd told her that he'd never wanted to be married in the first place.

She hadn't even been introduced to the public, Olivia thought sickly. And, if Khalil had renounced his claim, he would have let Elena go. Aziz could marry Elena, if he wanted to. If he wanted to be married at all.

She licked her lips, felt her heart beat with slow, hard, painful thuds. 'Do you…do you want to annul the marriage?'

'Annul?' Aziz turned around, his expression still so very blank. 'Is that what you want, Olivia?'

'I'm asking because you seem so…so strange, Aziz. And I know you never wanted to be married in the first place.'

'No,' he agreed after a moment. 'I didn't.'

'So…' She spread her hands, not wanting to be the one to say the words. She didn't want to offer him an out. Only hours ago she'd wanted to tell him she loved him. She'd wanted *more*, not less.

She still wanted more.

'So?' he repeated. 'So you want me to release you from our marriage vows? Is that it?' His voice rose, surprising both of them. 'So much for taking them seriously, then.'

'I thought it's what you wanted!' Olivia cried, her voice breaking. 'Tell me what you want, Aziz.'

He stared at her, his chest heaving with emotion, his eyes full of anguish she didn't understand. 'I want you to love me,' he whispered. 'God, I'd never thought I'd say that again. I never thought I'd let myself beg for someone's love ever again.'

'You don't need to beg—'

'But after I left you to see Khalil I realised how much I wanted you with me. How much I loved you.'

Olivia blinked back tears, amazement and hope unfurling inside her. 'You did?'

'Yes. I love you, Olivia, so much. I've been fighting it since you came to Kadar or, hell, maybe even before then. Maybe since I first started wondering about you, about the woman with the wonderful laugh who played music that made me want to both weep and sing. I just haven't wanted to tell you, haven't wanted to admit it even to myself, because it was so frightening to think of being rejected again—and this time even worse.'

'You wouldn't—' Olivia began, but he continued, the words coming faster.

'I don't expect you to love me back. I'm not asking for a miracle. But I needed to tell you, and I hope—' His voice wavered before he continued. 'I hope that maybe in time you might come to feel for me as I feel for you. At least a little.'

'Oh, Aziz.' A tear slipped down Olivia's cheek as she realised how much this beautiful, broken man was risking for her. He'd told her he loved her without any idea of how she felt in return. Without even hoping that she might love him the way he loved her.

He loved her.

'Is that too much to ask?' he whispered. 'In time? I know you've been hurt, Olivia. So badly. But I want to help you get over that pain, at least as much as you can. I'd never minimise how much losing Daniel affected you, but—'

'Aziz.' She smiled through her tears as she walked towards him. 'Stop talking.'

'What—?'

'I love you,' she said simply. 'I already love you. Now, here, so much. I wanted to tell you earlier but I didn't have the chance, and the truth is I was afraid you wouldn't want to hear it. Afraid of what I'd do, how I'd feel, if you told me you didn't want my love.'

Aziz was staring at her as if he couldn't make sense of her words. 'But a few minutes ago you asked if I wanted to annul our marriage.'

'Because I was *afraid*.' She knew she needed to explain more. 'I didn't tell you everything about when I gave up Daniel,' she began. 'Or just how badly it affected me.' She closed her eyes for a second, heard her father's determinedly cheerful voice in her head. *Do what your mother says, Olivia, it's for the best. Now, come on, darling, let's have no more unpleasantness. Play the piano for me, eh? Just like old times.*

As if she hadn't just spilled her guts right there in front of him, torn out her heart and offered it to him, begging him to help her. Support her.

It had been that fear, the memory of how hurt she'd been, how *destroyed* after confessing her heart, that had kept her from telling Aziz she loved him. But she was telling him now. She'd tell him everything.

'I told my father about Daniel,' she went on quietly. 'I asked, I *begged* him to support me. Sort of like you begged your father to love you, Aziz. And my father, my adored father, turned away from me. He didn't want to know. He didn't even want to look at me. And when I pleaded with him to help me keep my baby he just patted my head and told me to do what my mother said.' Her voice cracked. 'And then he asked me to play the piano for him.' She shook her head, half-amazed that such an old memory could still hurt so much. 'And you know what I did right then?' she finished sadly.

'You played the piano,' Aziz said softly and she nodded jerkily. 'It's what I would have done. What I *have* done, trying endlessly to please someone who didn't care about me. Trying to earn his love a thousand times over.' He reached for her then, pulled her into his arms and buried his face in her hair. 'When you asked if I wanted to annul the marriage I felt as if you'd just yanked my heart right out of my chest. I was trying to work up the courage to tell you I loved you—'

'And I made you think I wanted out. I'm sorry, Aziz.'

'We've both let old fears and hurts control our actions,' Aziz said, holding her tightly. 'But not any more. This is a new start for both of us, Olivia.'

'I want that. I want that so much.'

He eased back, framing her face with his hands as he gazed down at her. 'Tell me what happened after you told your father.'

She swallowed past the tightness in her throat. 'I did what he said. I went to the clinic and gave up my baby. And then I went to university and pretended nothing was wrong.' She still remembered how surreal it had felt, going to lectures and writing essays as if her world hadn't fallen right off its axis. Her stomach had been saggy, milk still leaking from her breasts just three weeks after giving birth. And she'd been in a fog, pretending it was normal, that she was okay. 'When I went home for Christmas, my parents acted as if nothing had happened,' she told Aziz. 'They seemed so jolly, pretending this was a normal Christmas. Or maybe they weren't even pretending. Maybe they really believed it was.'

'People believe what they want to believe,' he reminded her quietly. 'You told me you knew that was true. Were you thinking of them?'

'Yes.' She sniffed, let out another shuddering breath. 'I flew back to England and took a train to my university, but when it was time to get off I just didn't. I stayed on the train until the last stop and ended up in a run-down seaside town. I got a job working in a bed and breakfast for a while, then kept moving from place to place over the years, just existing. Anything to keep from feeling.'

'But you feel now.'

'I feel so much, and you made that happen, Aziz. You're like Prince Charming, waking me up with a kiss.'

He kissed her then, sweetly and softly. 'And you woke me up, Olivia. You took away my mask and kept me from hiding myself. My fears. And you believed in me, even when I didn't believe in myself.'

'Do you believe now, Aziz? Because I know you'll be a good ruler. A wonderful ruler.' She gazed at him seriously. 'Malik told me when I first arrived in Kadar that you didn't believe the people would support you. I see now it's because you haven't given them the chance.'

'I've been afraid to,' Aziz admitted quietly.

'You need to give them that chance, Aziz. I think you'll be surprised at how they take it.'

He lifted her hand and pressed a kiss to her palm. 'With you by my side, I feel like I can do anything.'

She reached up on her tiptoes and kissed him. 'You can,' she said. 'We can.'

Together, she knew, they could do anything.

EPILOGUE

Sᴜɴ sᴛʀᴇᴀᴍᴇᴅ ᴛʜʀᴏᴜɢʜ the palace windows as Olivia gave her reflection one last final check. Nerves fluttered in her stomach, but excitement did too. It had been six weeks since her wedding to Aziz and they were making a formal appearance on the balcony of the palace in Siyad, along with Khalil and Elena.

As soon as they'd left the coastal palace, Aziz had issued a press statement announcing the news. There had been a few whispers, a few raised eyebrows, but things were thankfully starting to settle down. When people had realised he and Olivia loved each other, just as Khalil and Elena did, they'd been enchanted. There were two happily-ever-afters instead of one.

Aziz had made Khalil his chief advisor and together they'd travelled around Kadar, visiting the desert tribes, sowing loyalty and support rather than discord.

The country was becoming united. Strong.

The door opened and Aziz stood there, smiling with an ease and sincerity that shone out of him. No longer the Gentleman Playboy, his charm was still devastating and not a mask. He was his real, wonderful self...just as she was. Aziz had helped her to recapture her hope, her joy. He'd brought out the best in her, made her see and feel the happiness and wonder of life again, and for that she would always be thankful.

Together they made each other stronger and more whole. *Complete.*

'Ready?' he asked. 'They're waiting for us to go out.'

'What about Khalil and Elena?'

'They're waiting, too.'

Khalil and Elena, Olivia knew, were just as happy as she and Aziz were. They divided their time between Thallia and Kadar and, if Olivia wasn't mistaken, they would be making an announcement about a future prince or princess some time soon.

Just as she hoped to, one day.

She slid her hand into Aziz's and they left the room for the salon that led to the palace's main balcony. Khalil and Elena were already there, heads bent together as Khalil whispered in Elena's ear. She giggled and smiled and Olivia's heart swelled with the happiness she knew they all felt.

Aziz and Khalil had found a solid, working relationship; they'd become allies and perhaps even friends. Almost brothers—bound by so much, if not by blood.

And Olivia liked Elena; they'd become friends too, as well as sisters-in-law of a sort.

'Ready?' Aziz said and everyone nodded. Olivia could feel the expectation in the room, the tension in Aziz. This was the first time they would all be appearing together in public.

An aide threw open the doors to the balcony and Olivia stepped out with Aziz, both of them blinking in the bright sunlight.

Below them the palace courtyard was thronged with people and the noise was incredible. They were chanting, Olivia realised, although it took a few seconds for her to realise what they were saying.

Sheikh Aziz! Sheikh Aziz!

She turned to her husband with a radiant smile. 'They love you,' she said softly, and he smiled back.

'They love us both. Shall we satisfy them?' She nodded and he drew her towards him for a kiss of both promise and thanksgiving, the sweetest kiss she'd ever known.

On her other side Khalil and Elena had come out, and they were both smiling and waving to the crowds.

Drawing back, his heart in his eyes, Aziz kept his hand tightly in hers as he turned to address his people.

* * * * *

If you enjoyed this book,
don't miss Khalil's story in
CAPTURED BY THE SHEIKH by Kate Hewitt

#3281 REBEL'S BARGAIN
The Chatsfield
by Annie West

Injured in a skiing accident, there's only one person Orsino can turn to...his estranged wife, Poppy. They have unfinished business, and as the blazing passion between them reignites, Orsino's left wondering—will Poppy's sensual touch kill...or cure?

#3282 A VIRGIN FOR HIS PRIZE
Ruthless Russians
by Lucy Monroe

Romi Grayson once infiltrated Maxwell Black's cast-iron defenses then walked away. Now this Russian tycoon will stop at nothing, even blackmail, to have Romi warm and willing in his bed. And her innocence will make his long-awaited possession even sweeter....

#3283 PROTECTING THE DESERT PRINCESS
Alpha Heroes Meet Their Match
by Carol Marinelli

Princess Layla craves escape from her gilded cage—she wants to experience *everything* forbidden! The exception? She must remain pure for her future husband. Mikael Romanov swore to protect her, but as Layla gets beneath his skin can Mikael protect her from himself?

#3284 TO DEFY A SHEIKH
by Maisey Yates

It isn't the first time Sheikh Ferran has faced the edge of an assassin's blade, but soon his beautiful assailant is at his mercy. Now Princess Samarah Al-Azem must decide: imprisonment in a cell...or in diamond shackles as the sheikh's wife!

HPCNM1014RA

#3285 THE VALQUEZ SEDUCTION
The Playboys of Argentina
by Melanie Milburne
When Argentinian polo player Luiz Valquez rescues innocent Daisy Wyndham, the press reports they're engaged! It's a dangerous charade: with Luiz doing his best to be good and Daisy trying to be bad, how long before someone gives in?

#3286 ONE NIGHT WITH MORELLI
by Kim Lawrence
Eve Curtis is determined to remain independent and is happy keeping men at a safe distance. Until now. Because when Draco Morelli sweeps her off her feet, he opens her eyes to a whole new world of sin and seduction....

#3287 THE RUSSIAN'S ACQUISITION
by Dani Collins
Alesky Dmitriev's revenge plans backfire when he discovers that his new mistress, Clair Daniels, is a virgin! Undeterred, he's set on enjoying the perks of his purchase. Clair, however, is destined to be much more than just this Russian's acquisition.

#3288 THE TRUE KING OF DAHAAR
A Dynasty of Sand and Scandal
by Tara Pammi
Nikhat Zakhari's desertion once drove Prince Azeez to recklessness, but now he must choose: spend life in the shadows of the past, or embrace his future. He *must* assume the crown—but will Nikhat agree to be his desert queen?

REQUEST YOUR
FREE BOOKS!

2 FREE NOVELS PLUS
2 FREE GIFTS!

YES! Please send me 2 FREE Harlequin Presents® novels and my 2 FREE gifts (gifts are worth about $10). After receiving them, if I don't wish to receive any more books, I can return the shipping statement marked "cancel." If I don't cancel, I will receive 6 brand-new novels every month and be billed just $4.30 per book in the U.S. or $4.99 per book in Canada. That's a saving of at least 14% off the cover price! It's quite a bargain! Shipping and handling is just 50¢ per book in the U.S. and 75¢ per book in Canada.* I understand that accepting the 2 free books and gifts places me under no obligation to buy anything. I can always return a shipment and cancel at any time. Even if I never buy another book, the two free books and gifts are mine to keep forever.

106/306 HDN FVRK

Name _____ (PLEASE PRINT) _____

Address _____ Apt. # _____

City _____ State/Prov. _____ Zip/Postal Code _____

Signature (if under 18, a parent or guardian must sign)

Mail to the **Harlequin® Reader Service:**
IN U.S.A.: P.O. Box 1867, Buffalo, NY 14240-1867
IN CANADA: P.O. Box 609, Fort Erie, Ontario L2A 5X3

**Are you a current subscriber to Harlequin Presents books
and want to receive the larger-print edition?
Call 1-800-873-8635 or visit www.ReaderService.com.**

* Terms and prices subject to change without notice. Prices do not include applicable taxes. Sales tax applicable in N.Y. Canadian residents will be charged applicable taxes. Offer not valid in Quebec. This offer is limited to one order per household. Not valid for current subscribers to Harlequin Presents books. All orders subject to credit approval. Credit or debit balances in a customer's account(s) may be offset by any other outstanding balance owed by or to the customer. Please allow 4 to 6 weeks for delivery. Offer available while quantities last.

Your Privacy—The Harlequin® Reader Service is committed to protecting your privacy. Our Privacy Policy is available online at www.ReaderService.com or upon request from the Harlequin Reader Service.

We make a portion of our mailing list available to reputable third parties that offer products we believe may interest you. If you prefer that we not exchange your name with third parties, or if you wish to clarify or modify your communication preferences, please visit us at www.ReaderService.com/consumerschoice or write to us at Harlequin Reader Service Preference Service, P.O. Box 9062, Buffalo, NY 14269. Include your complete name and address.

HPI3

"I would much rather find a way for you to be useful to me." He slid his thumb along the flat of her blade. "But where I could keep an eye on you, as I would rather this not end up in my back."

"I make no promises, sheikh."

"Again, we must work on your self-preservation."

"Forgive me, I don't quite believe I have a chance at it."

Something in Ferran's face changed, his eyebrows drawing tightly together. "Samarah."

He'd recognized her. At last. She'd hoped he wouldn't. Not when she was supposed to be dead. Not when he hadn't seen her since she was a child of six.

She met his eyes. "Sheikha Samarah Al-Azem, of Jahar. A princess with no palace. And I am here for what is owed me."

"You think that is blood, little Samarah?"

"You will not call me little. I just kicked you in the head."

"Indeed you did, but to me, you are still little."

"Try such insolence when I have my blade back, and I will cut your throat, sheikh."

"Noted," he said, regarding her closely. "You have changed."

"I ought to have. I'm no longer six."

"I cannot give you blood," he said. "For I am rather attached to having it in my veins, as you can well imagine."

"Self-preservation is something of an instinct."

"For most," he said, drily.

"Different when you have nothing to lose."

"And is that the position you're in?"

"Why else would I invade the palace and attempt an assassination? Obviously I have no great attachments to this life."

His eyes flattened, his jaw tightening. "I cannot give you blood, Samarah. But you feel you were robbed of a legacy. Of a palace. And that, I can perhaps see you given."

"Can you?"

"Yes. I have indeed thought of a use for you. By this time next week, I shall present you to the world as my intended bride."

* * *

Don't miss
TO DEFY A SHEIKH,
available November 2014.